TE DOMINION: TRUTH

GAVIN TEAGUE

A SELF-PUBLISHED NOVEL
PRINTED BY CREATESPACE

This is a work of fiction. All the characters and events portrayed in this book are fictional, and any resemblance to real people or incidents is purely coincidental.

TOOLS OF DOMINION: TRUTH

© Copyright 2014 Gavin Teague
All rights reserved.

First printing: September 2014

Published by Gavin Teague

Cover art design by Gavin Teague
Using images from Dreamstime Stock Photos (http://www.dreamstime.com/) &
Stock Free Images (http://www.stockfreeimages.com/)
Source image of armor used in front cover design ©Depositphotes.com/greglith

ISBN: 978-1500222529

Printed by CreateSpace, An Amazon.com Company

To all those who encouraged me to write
and gave me the confidence to publish this book

Prologue

Plans at Twilight

The winter sun set over New Babel Academy, spilling forth its final rays of light. The crisp mountain air made the light seem palpable, yet tenuous, like fragile strands of flaxen hair slowly retreating up the tall tower at the center of the campus. The light desperately clung to the structure before being abruptly cut off by the coming night. The earth itself seemed to reach up and drag the sun down into the surrounding snowcapped mountains.

A smile came to the lips of the woman looking out from the tower. She loved to see the moment the day died. The pain she felt in her eyes before the sun's retreat made the night's victory seem more personal, as if her own battle would also be won in the end.

Yes, it is inevitable, the woman mused. *The world is wasted on the ignorant masses. They go about their daily lives completely unaware of their own failings. But soon those unworthy pretenders to the throne of dominion will be put in their place.* The woman narrowed her eyes in contempt. *If only one of their guardians hadn't caught wind of my plans.*

A vexed sigh escaped the woman's lips as she returned to her desk. She appeared in her early thirties, with a tall, slender yet full body that would turn anyone's head. Her manner of walking showed a poise that hinted at her grace and charisma, advantages she had used to gain the trust and backing of many of the influential leaders in the worlds of business and politics. Even those that had, at first glance, foolishly considered her no more than a treat for the eyes soon came to realize she was an extremely competent and capable woman.

She had used the trust she'd earned to establish New Babel Academy as an educational facility for the future leaders of the world. Funded in large part by the United Nations, its official purpose was to foster an understanding between the elite of many nations in order to secure global peace and prosperity. Of course, the woman had ensured the bureaucrats had little involvement or oversight in the operation of the academy despite the funding received from the UN. It was an arrangement that would hold true so long as the academy produced its intended results.

Classes were held year round, though as long as performance maintained the highest levels of excellence, attendance was not required. Such provisions had been necessary for some of the students who were required to take part in their influential families' functions and activities. However, the academy still required all students to live in the campus boarding facilities, only allowing return trips home during breaks or with special permission. New Babel Academy was treated much like an independent nation. It was free from the restrictions and regulations a normal school would have endured. It served as a haven that allowed the students to enjoy some semblance of a normal school life compared to what they would otherwise have to expect.

Despite the forced separation from their children,

most parents strongly supported sending their children to New Babel Academy for two reasons. The first reason being the ease of and freedom to network with other children from influential families all over the world without the threat of political or social implications. The second reason, and perhaps the more important, was the academy's focus on providing real world lessons in management and the uses of power.

In line with this focus, the school was largely governed by the student body, with the Student Council holding even more power than the faculty. The only person who could overturn the Student Council's decisions was the founder and chairwoman of the academy. The same woman who now sat at her desk on the top floor of the academy's tower, glaring at the report set out in front of her.

The chairwoman had spent a great deal of time orchestrating events and manipulating people to get her grand project established, and now it was in its final stages. However, recent events had put everything in jeopardy. The woman grimaced as she read the report in front of her a second time. She didn't really need to read it again, but it was helping to focus her thoughts, so she continued. The contents explained that several people had fallen into comas over the past few months and showed no signs of improvement. They were all students of the academy. No one was sure what to make of the situation, and the chairwoman wasn't in a position to reveal the truth, but she knew.

The children would never awaken from their comas. They were nothing more than empty shells now, not really even fit to be called people. She had known right away they had been victims of attacks by a being consigned to myth: a psychic vampire. Of course, she couldn't reveal that fact to anyone. Even if she wanted to expose the attacker to the world, no one would believe her. So far, she had managed to cover up the attacks by speaking privately with the families of the students, but it would only be a matter of time before there were more victims.

The chairwoman also knew who the perpetrator was. She pulled out another file containing a dossier on the academy's doctor who resided on campus with the students. The doctor, Trish Vaashti, had been hired by the school staff at the beginning of the school year, about eight months ago now. She enjoyed immense popularity from the student body, so the chairwoman couldn't just dismiss the doctor without good reason due to the prominent role students played in the administration of the school.

She knew most of the background information on Trish would be falsified, and she couldn't act against the psychic vampire personally because it would be precisely what the vampire wanted. The fact Trish had used her real surname, Vaashti, made it obvious she was making no effort to hide her identity. The name was ancient, though only a few would recognize it. It tied her to one of the six great houses that protected and guided the world over four thousand years ago.

She must be trying to either lure me out, or shut down the academy. The chairwoman continued to think through the facts. *Or rather, she's trying to draw out the master here. If she knew my true nature she would have attacked me directly already, so my own identity is safe for the moment, but that doesn't help the other problem. If I can't provide better protection for the children it will only be a matter of time before the world loses faith in the academy and my plans will be ruined.*

A second sigh escaped the woman's lips. The only conclusion she had come up with would be difficult to implement, and would definitely slow down her plan, but there was no alternative. Keeping the school open was the highest priority. She almost wanted to laugh at her own frustration when she thought about the situation. *So this is what it feels like to protect others while hiding yourself. I never would have imagined my plans would reverse the roles between the psychic vampires and myself. I never imagined they would have caught wind of what was going on here so quickly.*

At least the chairwoman had come to a short term solution to her problem, though it would only delay dealing with the cause. She was about to reach for the phone when the sound of footsteps reached her ears. From the sound, the chairwoman knew exactly when the visitor was close enough to knock on the door.

"Enter," she commanded before the footsteps had even come to a stop.

The door immediately swung open and a teenage boy stepped three paces into the room then bowed. Neither of them was surprised. The boy had expected the woman to be aware of his approach, and the woman knew who the visitor was before the door had opened. Conveniently, this boy was the one the chairwoman had been about to call: the Student Council President.

"My lady, I have been going over the background checks on the admissions applicants that passed the entrance exam and I found one you might consider interesting," the president reported to explain his presence.

The woman quirked an eyebrow. "Oh, it's unusual for you to bring me an issue which is clearly within the jurisdiction of the student body. I'll have a look in a moment, but first I was about to inform you of a decision I've made."

The president glanced at the chairwoman's desk, seeing the files still open on it. "Does this have to do with that woman and the coma patients?" the boy practically snarled.

"Calm yourself." The chairwoman narrowed her eyes at the boy. "As I've told you before, she is beyond your ability to deal with. Do not do anything that can give your true nature away, and on that note, I want you to pass these instructions down to the others. All our children are required to take additional classes to learn how to avoid detection and to defend themselves if they are attacked. They will no longer be permitted to travel alone. Also, no more siring is permitted unless the potential sire can demonstrate their mastery of the additional class material and are able to instruct their child."

The president's eye widened. "But my lady, that could slow our growth rate by months for each new generation. Can the plan be slowed that much?"

The chairwoman scoffed, "It isn't like we don't have time. Even if Trish Vaashti hadn't come it would have taken at least a decade for the plans to come to fruition." The woman softened her tone as she continued, "Besides, this is only a temporary measure until we can find a more effective way to deal with the girl."

The boy frowned. "I don't see why we don't all just attack her at once."

The chairwoman shook her head. "I've told you she is beyond you. I mean it. You are still too young to even comprehend the powers one like her actually holds. Even if we gathered all our children together, they'd just be food for her. That's why you must all learn how to defend yourselves first. We'll see what options we have after that. Now, what was this other matter you came to see me about."

The Student Council President bowed in acceptance before advancing to the desk. He held out a folder containing a dossier of a potential student named

Theron Zeyla. The chairwoman took the folder and scanned the contents.

The woman's eyes widened in surprise. "A perfect score on the application test?"

The student nodded. "Yes, but that's not why I brought you the document."

The chairwoman didn't acknowledge the statement because she already knew as much and had continued reading the background of the applicant. "So this boy has lived in an orphanage for the past six years. Before that he lived with his parents, Felecia and Renaud Zeyla." The chairwoman paused, recalling the names. "I remember them. They were two well-liked and respected diplomats working in West Germany before they fell in love and decided to start a family. Both were the sole heirs to their own elite families as I recall, making this boy the heir apparent to a rather large fortune. I imagine due to his age at the time he wasn't allowed to be the executor of his parents' estate, but being sent to an orphanage? It's rather hard to imagine no arrangements had been made, especially since the cause of their death was an unidentified wasting disease. It wasn't sudden at all."

"I had found that curious as well, so I did some more research," the president explained. "Apparently the will left behind by Theron Zeyla's parents designated the orphanage he was to be raised by, and set forth provisions to reimburse the headmaster of the orphanage for expenses related to raising Theron. The terms sounded reasonable enough, but I'm still surprised such elite parents would allow their child to be raised in an orphanage after they were gone."

The chairwoman tilted her head to the side, a habit she showed while thinking on something puzzling. She had never stopped reading the dossier, and was now almost done with it. "This is fascinating. The boy was born with a very weak body, so weak the doctors thought he would die soon after birth, but not only did he pull through, but by the time he started attending school he was the most physically gifted in his class. Meanwhile, his parents had already contracted the disease which slowly robbed them of their own strength until their bodies finally gave out." She grinned as she continued, "It's hard to believe everyone wrote that off as a tragic twist of fate, but it works to our advantage now." The woman closed the folder and handed it back to the president as new plans formed in her mind. "Admit Theron Zeyla into the school as a special scholarship student."

The president bowed as he accepted the folder. "It shall be as you command, my lady. In this and in all things." The boy then turned and walked out of the room.

A smile once again came to the lips of the chairwoman as she sat at her desk. *A naturally born psychic vampire, unknown to his own kind, to mold as my protégé. This could finally be the turning point in our long war. Theron Zeyla could be both the perfect distraction for Trish Vaashti and the strongest weapon to use against her. I'll have to arrange events carefully over the next few months before young Theron arrives.*

Campus Layout

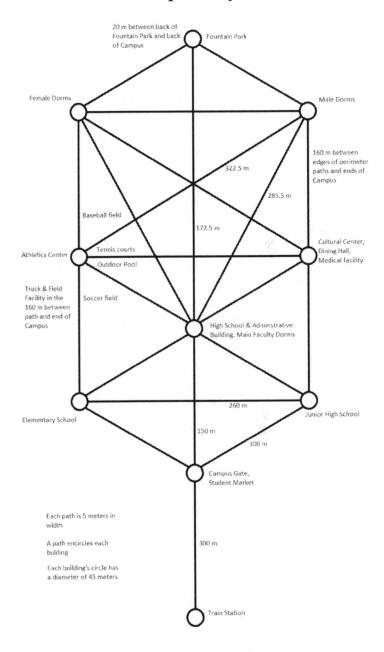

Chapter 1

The Special Scholarship Student

"Attention passengers. We will be arriving at New Babel Academy Station in ten minutes. Please prepare to disembark." The announcement woke several people up, and the quiet train car began to bustle with activity as people started to gather their belongings.

One person, though also awakened by the announcement, didn't show any signs of moving yet. The sixteen year old boy didn't have anything to gather. It was a subtle reminder that he didn't really fit in with the people around him. The boy grimaced as he looked at his clothes. They were a much less subtle reminder that he didn't belong among the people around him. The dark slacks, white short-sleeve dress shirt, and crimson tie were the best clothes he had, but anyone could tell they were cheap quality when compared to the clothes the other passengers on the train wore. The boy forced himself to stop thinking about the ways he didn't fit in. He turned his attention to the papers he had held in his hand the entire trip. The documents verified his admission into New Babel Academy.

The first sheet of paper in his hand was a letter congratulating him, Theron Zeyla, on being the special admittance scholarship student for the new term. It was embossed with the crest of the school on it, an image depicting a sword with drops of blood falling from it, with a hilt wrapped in roses. The crest was supposed to bring together the ideas of beauty, power, and bloodlines. It seemed a fitting crest for a school catering to the elite. Theron gently rubbed the crest with his thumb. The action was a slight betrayal of the calm demeanor he projected to mask the excitement he felt each time he looked at the letter. That letter marked his first real step towards reaching his goal.

Theron slowly turned his gaze away from the paper to look out the window. The train had just made it out of a tunnel. The whole area was shaded by the surrounding mountains. The ground was fairly dark, as if there were storm clouds blocking the sun, but Theron could still see a clear blue sky when he looked up. *So this is what spring in the mountains is like*, Theron thought to himself. *It looks like there won't be much direct sunlight. Thank God for that.*

Theron didn't exactly hate sunlight, but whenever he had to go out during the day he had to keep his gaze down and squint to guard against the blinding light. It seemed his eyes were very sensitive, and they couldn't quite adjust properly to the brightness of the sun no matter how long he was exposed to it.

He shifted his attention to the other children aboard the train. The new school year for the academy started in three days, so the train was full of students returning from home. In contrast, going to school was a kind of homecoming for Theron. It was his first step back into the world of his parents.

When he thought of it that way, the fact that Theron didn't really fit in with the elite children around him didn't sting quite so much. He may not belong here yet, but there had been a time when he was a part of the elite society, and Theron was determined to reclaim that position. Over the past six years, spent in an orphanage following his parents' death, he had slowly been stripped of almost everything, but it was only in the past year he had come to learn the depths of betrayal he was suffering at the hands of those who should have been caring for him. Now he was finally in a position to begin fighting back and reclaim what was rightfully his. This was his new beginning. A small smile finally crept onto his lips as his excitement continued to rise.

"Oh, that's a cute smile."

Theron's expression became blank as his attention was immediately drawn to his surroundings. He noticed a girl sitting across the aisle looking at him. She must have been the one who spoke.

"I'm sorry. I didn't mean to startle you, the words just slipped out. I don't really know why, but my eyes have been drawn to you this whole trip, but I didn't want to disturb you while you appeared to be sleeping." The girl averted her eyes slightly as a faint blush colored her cheeks.

Theron couldn't help but be a little captivated by the expression. She was a beautiful girl, with radiant, rich red hair that reached halfway down her back and ended in cute ringlets. She wasn't particularly tall. Theron guessed the top of her head would probably only reach his nose, but she had very nice proportions. She also had vibrant green eyes. Her smile was radiant, managing to be cute, charming and genuine all at the same time. He knew he couldn't just keep staring at her, so he said the first thing which came to mind. "I'm not the one that's cute."

The girl's eyes widened a bit at the compliment before she showed a bright smile and giggled in a wonderfully feminine way that reminded Theron of little bells softly ringing out, spreading happiness. "It's nice to meet you," the girl said. "I haven't seen you in the school before. Are you a new student?"

Theron nodded. "I was accepted this past January. I'm enrolled as a second year high school student."

"Oh, so we're in the same year!" The girl sounded very happy about that. "My name is Katerina Aikia. I hope we'll be able to get along." The girl gave her best smile yet.

"I would like that very much. My name is Theron Zeyla." Theron paused for a moment, considering the girl's name. "I think the name suits you; it's a wonderful name."

Katerina blushed and stared at Theron for a moment before she began to speak in a rush to hide her embarrassment. "Oh, well, it isn't my real name of course. Well, Katerina is, but I picked out the name Aikia when I enrolled. Come to think of it, you may not know this yet because you're new, but since the students here are children of people with influence in the world, we take on false names to protect our identities. Since this school is about making genuine relationships with others, hiding our family name and status allows us to have more trust in others. We can be sure our friendships aren't built solely on family status. Of course, the school administration still knows our real names, and it's not unusual for students to know each other outside of school either. However, picking different family names is also symbolic of our family status not holding sway in the school, so we're free to live relatively normal lives. It's actually a luxury for many of us."

"I suppose that would be nice for an elite. As for me, my parents' position wouldn't mean anything, so there's no real harm in using my real name." Theron's face clouded over a bit as he was reminded again of what he had lost. *If my parents had never died, would I have been able to understand this girl a little better? Would I be able to appreciate living a so-called normal life?*

"Your parents' position?" Katerina paused to think about Theron's words before suddenly getting excited as she seemed to come to a realization. "Are you the special scholarship student?"

"Huh? Yes I am, why?" Theron was puzzled over the reaction. Was it really such a big deal?

"That's amazing!" Katerina exclaimed. "Only one student is offered the scholarship in a year, and there have been several years since the school's founding in which it wasn't given out at all. Receiving it is basically like being acknowledged as a true elite. Not someone born to status, but someone with the talents necessary to climb to the top on their own. Oh my God, I never thought I'd be lucky enough to get to know a special scholarship student! And you're not arrogant about it at all. I guess true geniuses really are different."

Theron had figured out this girl was the easily excitable type earlier, but the latest barrage of hyper enthusiasm was overwhelming. He had no idea his scholarship meant so much more than a simple fully paid admittance. He wasn't sure how to respond. Luckily a lurch caused by the train's final braking broke his feeling of awkward tension.

"Attention passengers, we have arrived at New Babel Academy Station. Please disembark in an orderly manner. Porters will gather your stowed luggage for you and take it to your assigned rooms. We hope you have had a pleasant journey with us."

Katerina stood up and walked across the aisle to Theron, holding out her hand with a smile. "Shall I escort you to the dormitory?"

Theron took her hand to appease her, though he didn't put much pressure on it as he stood up. They proceeded to disembark as Theron said, "Normally I would love to have you escort me, but according to my papers I'm supposed to go meet the chairwoman of the academy as soon as I arrive. If you could point me to her office, I'd be most appreciative."

"Oh, the administration building is that tower rising above the high school." Katerina pointed out towards the campus ahead of them as they walked. A tower that looked to be about three hundred fifty meters in height reached up into the sky in front of them. "It's the central building on campus. It's attached to the high school and also serves as the main faculty dormitory. All the other buildings have pathways to it, so how about I walk with you on my way to the girls' dormitory?"

Theron had no reason to refuse her, so he nodded his head, and began walking beside her. The path towards the campus extended ahead of them from the train station for three hundred meters until it came to an enormous gate house. It rose up over ten meters into the air, with thick walls and a tunnel that seemed to extend about fifteen meters in length. It had a massive black iron portcullis which stood open about three meters in height and five meters in width. The gate gave off the impression of swallowing up all the arriving students. Extending on either side of the gate house was a kind of hybrid wall and fence, with granite stone forming a series of arches that held iron spikes spaced about ten centimeters apart. It gave a mixed impression of a fortress and a high class estate's security fence. Theron also noted the stonework was made from a single piece of stone, as if the entire gatehouse and wall had been carved out from the mountain rather than being built.

Katerina kindly began explaining everything Theron was seeing, acting as his tour guide. "The security fence and gate remain closed during the school term. Only students with special permission may leave the campus during the term. It also prevents unauthorized guests from entering the campus. The gate house is fully staffed by campus security, and they also have a barracks there.

"All this area used to be a mountain, but they removed the overburden of the entire area and leveled it, carving out most of the buildings as they dug down. The only exception is the tower. There were concerns about the structural integrity given its height, so it's a relatively thin outer shell of stone reinforced by a steel framework underneath. The inside of the tower is walled with marble panels. Of course it's not like any of the buildings are bare rock on the inside either. They've been decorated with various kinds of panels. I've heard they chose paneling that could be easily changed to suit the tastes of occupants. My own room in the dorms uses rosewood panels.

"Beyond the gate you'll find the student market. Authorized merchants are allowed to set up shops and sell them to students. Some students also create stalls for themselves and sell their goods and services to other students. The market closes an hour before the dormitories lock their doors. It's not actually a curfew, but most students don't really stay out later than that."

Katerina finally ended her explanation, but she seemed to be fidgeting a bit and frequently glancing at him as they walked together. Theron guessed she was bothered by his silence, or maybe she was worried she had talked too much. Theron hid an amused grin that almost showed on his lips. He decided the best way to put her at ease would be to make a comment. "I'm surprised there are so many trees growing if this was once a mountain."

Katerina blinked in surprise at Theron's comment.

"Oh, I totally forgot about that. All the ground around the pathways are cut five meters deeper and filled with fertilized soil. Apparently there are even heaters installed to keep the ground from getting too cold. The trees and grass were all planted by landscapers. Some of the areas between paths even have small lakes in them with boats you can row out in and just sit on the water. The grounds are really beautiful. Maybe we can explore them together some day?" She looked over at him, her eyes almost begging for an answer.

"I think that sounds like a nice idea. But hearing all that makes me think this place must have been outrageously expensive to develop." Theron couldn't help feeling amazed by all the work and planning that must have gone into creating the campus.

"I'm sure it was, but that's also a sign of the respect and power commanded by the chairwoman," Katerina responded.

Theron could hear the respect in Katerina's voice, and he also thought he heard a hint of awe. It made him feel a bit apprehensive at his meeting with the chairwoman. The fact that the tower was now looming above him just a few paces away certainly didn't help. Theron stopped and looked up, trying to guess how tall the tower was. He gave up and turned to Katerina. "I guess we'll part here."

Katerina nodded and bit her lip. "If it's all right with you, could you come by the girls' dormitory after your meeting? I want to hear about how it went. You can just ask the dorm mother to call me down. I'll let her know I'm expecting you as well, so there won't be any problems."

Theron was a bit taken aback by the boldness of the girl's request. Katerina was trying awfully hard to be friends with him. It wasn't unusual for someone to become attached to him. In fact, Theron had been the one assigned to look after new children that got admitted to his orphanage because people tended to bond with him easily. However, Katerina's behavior seemed deeper than that. Theron found the neediness in her behavior a little troubling. He couldn't figure it out and now wasn't the time to be asking her. Besides, Theron had to admit he rather liked the attention even if he was troubled by what Katerina's reasons for giving it might be. Maybe he'd ask her about her reasons one day after they knew each other better, but for now he simply agreed to her request. "I'll stop by after the meeting."

Katerina smiled happily as she turned away. "I'll be waiting for you." She began walking on the circular path going around the building, heading clockwise. Theron watched her until she was out of sight before taking a deep breath and approaching the entrance to the high school building that also served as the entrance to the tower.

Once inside, the first things Theron saw were tables and chairs laid out in a room that was fifteen by ten meters. Some of the tables were big enough to seat ten people; others were more like private dining tables for two. Some chairs were stand-alone recliners. It looked like the entry room also served as a waiting room. A place where students who arrived early or stayed late could sit and relax, chat with other students, or maybe even read a book.

There was a large, five meter wide, archway that led to the next room. That room only contained a spiral staircase in the approximate center and a few elevators on the sides of the room. Theron thought about the position of the staircase relative to the tower that rose out of the school building and realized it was actually significantly off center. He concluded the top floors must be almost exclusively on one side of the tower even though on this floor the stairs looked almost centered.

Past the staircase was another large archway going into a room filled with rows of lockers. Most of them were opened, still unassigned because the new term hadn't started. Each locker was a meter tall and thirty centimeters in width and depth. The rows were elevated off the ground about half a meter, making the tops of the lockers come up to about Theron's neck. The room was about fifteen meters by ten meters, containing ten rows of lockers and twenty lockers per row. That was more than twice as many lockers as there were students enrolled, but Theron remembered Katerina had told him the tower also served as the faculty dormitory, so the teachers probably used the lockers as well. Theron also noted a large exit leading to the back of the campus on the other side of the locker room.

As he entered the locker room, Theron saw hallways extending out to either side. There seemed to be a classroom on each side of each hallway. Each of the four classrooms was marked with a sign that displayed a number one and different letters: A through D. Theron concluded the classrooms were for the first year students. There were also stairs and restrooms at the end of each hallway.

Thinking about the layout, Theron realized he had technically entered through the back entrance compared to the entrance the students would normally use. The dormitories were at the back of the campus, so the locker room, which was on the dormitory side, would actually be the room the students entered first. As Theron was thinking, an adult came out of one of the classrooms and saw him.

"What are you doing in here? Classes don't start for three more days, and classroom tours for new students aren't until tomorrow." The man didn't sound particularly upset. If anything, the teacher sounded concerned, thinking maybe something was wrong.

"I'm here for a meeting with the chairwoman," Theron stated calmly, explaining his presence and trying to put the teacher at ease.

The man gave him a puzzled look. "The chairwoman? What could you have to speak with her about?"

Before Theron could respond, another voice answered from behind him. "He's here because of the instructions he received as the special scholarship student, Mr. Gurnam. I assume you are Theron?"

Theron had turned to face the other person when he spoke. He seemed about Theron's age, making him another student. The boy had dark hair, almost black. He was about Theron's height, one hundred seventy-eight centimeters. He wore a royal blue blazer that had the school's crest on it. The student had come down from the spiral staircase and advanced into the hallway to come into view of the teacher.

"Oh, President Cynan. So you're here to escort him then?" The teacher seemed to tense up when he saw the student. The boy nodded to the teacher in response.

"I take it you're the Student Council President? I am Theron Zeyla. I wasn't expecting such an important escort." Theron extended his hand in greeting.

"Please, call me Deacon, you and I are both students here, which makes us peers. Besides, you're a rare case even among special scholarship students." Deacon shook Theron's hand. "Now, I know you're probably nervous and in rush to get things over with, but the chairwoman isn't quite ready for the meeting yet, so I'll take the opportunity to give you an early tour of the building while we wait."

"All right." Theron nodded.

"There really isn't a whole lot to cover on the first

floor that you haven't already seen," Deacon began explaining, "The ground floor classrooms are for first years. The lockers are basically just for coats and umbrellas. Students don't move from classroom to classroom here. Instead, the teachers rotate to teach each class. Since you'll be the only one sitting in the seat you'll be assigned to, you can feel free to leave the books you don't need there each day. The staircases on the far sides of each hallway go to the second and third floor. The central stairs and the elevators are the only way to get to the fourth floor, which acts as the faculty dorms, and the rooftop, which is generally only used by a few clubs, like the astronomy club. Of course, anything higher would be the tower itself, which can also only be accessed by the central stairs or the elevators."

Theron nodded at the explanation. After seeing the nod, Deacon began walking towards the spiral staircase that he had called the central stairs. Theron followed him to the second floor. The layout was the same as the first floor, but in place of a waiting room full of chairs and tables there was what looked like a grand restaurant's kitchen, with numerous stoves and dishwashers and a great deal of counter space. In place of the locker room was a showroom filled with pieces of art on display, each seemed to be accompanied by plaques or ribbons indicating all the pieces were award winning. There was also a huge trophy case filled with awards.

"As you can probably guess, the second floor has the same layout as the ground floor. We have the home economics room and the awards gallery on this floor. Also, the classrooms for this floor are for second year students, so this will be where you attend classes. Classroom placement is generally determined by a blend of academic performance, observed social prowess, and extracurricular activities. Since we don't have any real observations of your social interactions, you aren't eligible for Class A yet, so you'll be in Class 2-B, though I expect that to change in relatively short order. Because there are perks and rewards for being in a higher ranked class, we have a placement test system for those who want to advance. There are also competitions between classes which help students advance in rank," Deacon explained.

"So the most elite are in Class A, and the under achievers are in Class D. Of course, I expect the "under achievers" in this school would be superior to the top students of most other schools," Theron concluded.

"That's true." Deacon nodded. "In fact, all the awards in the gallery are from Class D. We don't allow the higher ranked classes to compete with other schools. Instead, they compete in open amateur and professional exhibitions and competitions so they can face stronger competition. The students generally keep those awards, so only the extramural awards are kept here. Of course, we still allow students from Class A through Class C to compete athletically, but that's purely part of extracurricular activities. Solo competition is required for the elective classes like art and music as part of the curriculum."

"Speaking of extracurricular activities, I don't see a gym, or even an art or a band room," Theron commented.

Deacon nodded again at Theron's observation. "Those facilities are housed in different areas on campus. The gym is part of the Athletics Center in the northwest, and the art and band classes are held in the Cultural Center to the northeast. In the grounds around the Athletics center you'll find the sports fields, tennis courts, and swimming pools. The Cultural Center also serves as the hub of social functions, so it has the dining hall, an auditorium, and a ballroom. The medical facility is also located there."

"It seems strange to put the medical facility with the Cultural Center." Theron pointed out.

Deacon let a little grin show on his face. "I didn't design the campus. I don't know why the chairwoman decided to lay things out the way she did, but I'm sure she has her reasons."

Theron let the topic go and indicated he was ready to move on with a shrug. The two continued up the stairs to the third floor. The layout of the rooms remained the same as the floors below, but this time, instead of a waiting room or a home economics room, there was a library. It wasn't all that large as far as libraries went, with probably only a few thousand books, but it appeared to specialize as a research library with a small computer lab in the center, probably for typing reports or searching the internet. The other side wasn't an open room like the locker room or the awards gallery, but instead was marked with a sign designating the Student Council offices.

Deacon resumed his explanation. "Obviously, on this floor we have the research library and the Student Council offices. This is also the floor for third year students. If you can't find something in the library here, check the library in the Cultural Center. If they don't have what you're looking for, they can get it for you. The library there also has a computer lab in it, so it's pretty convenient for research as well, though of course they have a lot of pleasure reading material too. If you have any questions or problems, you can feel free to come to the Student Council offices. Even if I'm not available, the other Student Council members should be able to help you. They're not here today, but they'll be introduced during the opening ceremony, so you'll be able to meet them soon."

"Okay, I'll look forward to it," Theron responded. "So, is it almost time to meet the chairwoman?"

"I think it'll be fine to go up now. We'll go ahead and take the elevator from here though, walking up a hundred flights of stairs isn't my idea of a good time." Deacon grinned.

"That sounds like a good idea," Theron agreed as he returned Deacon's smile.

Deacon led the way to the elevators and pressed the upward call button. Once the door opened and the two got on, Deacon took out a keycard. "Only authorized personnel have access to the chairwoman," he commented as he pressed the button for the top floor and swiped his keycard on the sensor at the bottom of the panel.

"Ah, so that's why you had to come escort me," Theron said as the elevator lurched, beginning it's ascent.

Deacon nodded. "Yeah, that and because I wanted to meet you ahead of time. As the Student Council President I try to make it a point to know all the students. Besides, given your status as a special scholarship student, it's likely that you'll become a local celebrity. I figure developing a mutually beneficial relationship might be in order."

Theron could feel the pressure building in his ears. Apparently they were rising at a relatively rapid pace. He swallowed to try to relieve some of the pressure before he asked, "What kind of mutually beneficial relationship?"

"Oh, we'll have to see how the situation develops, but who knows, maybe we'll be able to use your celebrity status to help make student functions more successful, and in return, if your fans start getting too demanding, we'll be able to provide some support and relief." Deacon shrugged as he gave a possible scenario

Tools of Dominion: Truth

off the top of his head.

At first, Theron didn't think Deacon's scenario was very plausible, but then he remembered Katerina's reaction to his scholarship status. *The president may have a point*, Theron thought to himself and decided not to comment. After about a minute, he could feel the elevator slowing as it neared the top of the tower.

Once the doors opened and the two stepped out of the elevator, Theron noted his earlier conclusion that the stairs would be to one side of the tower rather than centered was accurate. There was not an archway on each side leading to separate rooms on this floor. Instead the area they were in seemed to act as a kind of antechamber with a couple padded chairs and only one set of doors. Deacon walked up to the door and knocked.

"Enter," a voice rang out from beyond the door.

Deacon pushed open the doors and took three steps into the room, bowed, then turned to the side and held out a hand to indicate Theron. "Madam Chairwoman, I present to you Theron Zeyla, recipient of the special scholarship for the new term."

The chairwoman looked up from her desk. The slow rise of her head gave a feeling of gracefulness that flowed into her rise from her chair and continued on in her walk towards Theron. Theron was instantly captivated. He couldn't offer a bow. For a moment he couldn't even think enough to remember to breathe. He had thought Katerina was beautiful, but this woman made that kind of beauty seem a childish imitation. There was a gentle sway to her walk which accentuated her long legs, and her straight posture gave off an air of confidence. The chairwoman was tall. She didn't need to shift her gaze to look directly into Theron's eyes.

As she came closer, Theron's attention was drawn to her eyes. They were a red-violet color. It seemed an impossible shade for a human eye, but it gave her an otherworldly feel that felt so appropriate it had to be their genuine color. Her hair was a lustrous blonde that gleamed like fire in the setting sun. Theron was so enthralled he only now noticed they were high enough to still see the sun. From the lower floors the sun had already been hidden by the mountains. When the chairwoman stopped in front of Theron and held out her hand, he could only look at it dumbly for a few moments before he realized he should shake it.

The woman's eyes showed Theron she knew what he was feeling, and a smile showed up on her lips. It wasn't an energetic, cute smile like Katerina had shown him, but a calm, beautiful, and graceful smile. Somehow, even though the smile seemed genuine, it broke the spell over Theron. Even though it was a wonderful smile, for some reason Theron couldn't help comparing it to Katerina's smile and finding it a bit lacking. It made no sense to him, but he felt it was true. At least now he was able to speak.

"It's a pleasure to meet you, Madam Chairwoman. Thank you for accepting me into this academy," Theron tried to say it with as much calm gravity as he could, but his words sounded forced as his throat struggled to give them voice.

"The pleasure is mine, Theron Zeyla. Now, please forgive me if I seem rushed, but I need to ask a few questions to complete your admission and I don't have much time to spare, so if you would please have a seat. President Cynan, you may go." The chairwoman turned and began walking back to her desk. Theron saw Deacon bowing again to the chairwoman then returning to the elevator, closing the doors behind him. Theron followed the chairwoman and lowered himself gently into one of the chairs across from her. He sat silently, waiting for the first question.

"I understand you've been living in an orphanage. So tell me, why would a boy from an orphanage apply to a school for the most elite children in the world? I want the complete and honest answer." The chairwoman's eyes grabbed Theron's attention again, commanding obedience.

Theron couldn't resist. The words rolled off his tongue even though he had never voiced them to anyone before. "I came to this school to reclaim what should be mine, and to pay back the people who betrayed me. As you've said, I've been living in an orphanage for the past six years, but I am still my parents' child. I remember my parents telling me they used to be diplomats before I was born. They were both from wealthy families. Before they got sick, they would occasionally take me to high society parties. They raised me with care to be true elite. They wanted me to be the kind of person that used the power and influence I gained in life to help protect and improve the lives of the people around me. They were such wonderful parents, and I loved them so much.

"When they became ill, I watched them slowly wither away in front of me. Day after day, week after week, my parents' lives slowly slipped away. It was excruciating for me to watch the light slowly dull and fade from their kind, loving eyes. I remember they were able to have the best doctors brought in during those final few years. Those doctors called it a wasting disease, but only because there was no other term close enough to describe it. There was no evidence of any infection or toxins. It wasn't caused by a virus. It didn't appear to be contagious even though they both had the same symptoms. In the end, no one could even figure out what was causing their illness, much less help them. All I could do was watch as they continued to grow weaker and weaker. Then, a little over six years ago, I finally lost everything: my parents, my friends, my life."

Tears silently made their way down Theron's cheek, but he couldn't stop speaking. The chairwoman's eyes compelled him to continue. "After my parents died, the executor of the will they had made brought me to the orphanage and explained the terms. The orphanage was to care for me until I reached the age of majority, at which time I would gain full control over my parents' estate. Until that time, the orphanage would be able to use whatever funds they required for my upbringing from the estate. It all sounded very legitimate at first, but I slowly began to realize things weren't so straightforward."

Theron's tears had already dried, and his sorrow was being replaced by anger. His emotions shifted as he relived his memories. "I suppose the first odd thing I noticed was that whenever people would come in to see the children for adoption, I was always hidden away. It would be one thing if they had simply told people I couldn't be adopted due to my circumstances, but hiding me away began to make me suspicious. Then, a little over a year ago, I discovered what was really going on. On a day the executor was coming to see the headmaster of the orphanage, presumably to discuss monthly expenses and to ensure I was being treated well, I secretly listened in on their conversation.

"They were talking about authorizing reimbursements for doctors' fees on behalf of other orphans. They planned to use money from my parents' estate. It wasn't unusual for the children at that orphanage to become ill. Come to think of it, it's a little strange I myself never got sick while I was there. Anyway, I could rationalize them using my parents' money to pay for the other children's treatment as a preventative measure on my behalf, and honestly, I didn't really mind that part. However, after that they began talking about how much they should mark up the fees in the reports and still make it seem legitimate. They discussed what each of their cuts from the profit would be. They laughed about how brilliant their schemes were. They were taking extra money out of my parents' estate and using it to line their pockets.

"Then they began discussing what else they could do to finish draining my inheritance before I could turn eighteen. I realized they were intentionally robbing me and betraying my parents' trust in them. I was outraged, and nearly burst into the room then, but something stopped me. Maybe it was some premonition that made me realize that if these people could lie and cheat to that extreme, then they might do something even worse if I let on that I knew what was going on. I decided that I should keep quiet and focus on getting out of the orphanage as soon as I could. Then they would lose their excuse for siphoning money from my parents' estate. I decided the best step I could take would be to research and apply to multiple boarding schools.

"To be honest, I thought New Babel Academy was a long shot. As you said, this is an academy for the elite. I would be little more than a beggar in comparison, but then I remembered my parents' world. I remember the high society parties they would take me to when I was young, before they got too sick. Even after they couldn't travel anymore, I remember some of their friends visiting them. I remember mingling with the children of those people and having so much fun. I knew it was a long shot, but I figured I would give it a chance. Not only so I could get away from the orphanage, but also so I could try to get back into that world I remembered. That's why I had the audacity to apply to this school." Theron felt a pressure lift from him as he finally finished his story.

The chairwoman smiled kindly at Theron. It still didn't affect him as much as Katerina's had, but it affected him more than her previous smile had. "That is definitely a serious problem for a child, and I think you've demonstrated good judgment and great courage in how you're presently handling the situation, but I'm surprised the orphanage allowed you to come considering the circumstances."

"I never told them," Theron admitted. "I would have had to tell them if I was going to a different boarding school. Otherwise they could report me as a runaway and have the authorities take me back to the orphanage. However, this school operates as an independent nation as I understand it, and I could be given protection from any attempts they could make to try to force me to return to them."

The chairwoman nodded. "I see, and I will offer you that protection. This will probably be a surprise to you, but I knew your parents before they retired. When I saw your application and background I was shocked. I knew your parents had retired to focus on raising you, and given how much passion they had for their work they must have loved you dearly. I had wondered why you would have been sent to an orphanage when they themselves were so well loved and no doubt had friends who would have gladly taken you in. I simply can't see them leaving you to an orphanage."

"But the will clearly stated I was to be given to that orphanage. I read it myself," Theron protested.

"And the executor of the will was party to the scheme to defraud you of your inheritance." The chairwoman paused to let that fact sink in before continuing, "Obviously we have no evidence, but it wouldn't surprise me if the will was fake. The executor saw an opportunity of a lifetime to make a fortune off a ten year old boy who had no one left in the world to look after him. He probably did write up a legitimate will with your parents, but then later forged a fake will that would allow him to take advantage of you. Since he knew the details of what was actually supposed to happen, he probably took actions against whatever arrangements were already made. After all, if other arrangements had been made for your care, there must be another party that agreed to it."

Theron was shocked. The chairwoman made it sound so obvious. How did he not realize it before. The reason why they had to hide him when people came in to adopt children was because he wasn't supposed to be there at all. How could he have continued to believe the will was legitimate when the bearer had already proven untrustworthy?

The chairwoman stood up and came around her desk, kneeling down in front of Theron and taking his hand. "I can see your anger starting to take hold, but please put it aside if you can. You are now a student of New Babel Academy, and this is a relatively small issue in the world that awaits you. For the next two years, those two can't do anything more to you. I will personally begin taking some action on your behalf as well, so I want you to focus on enjoying your student life. Build relationships. Catch up on high society etiquette. Prepare for your return to the world you belong to."

Theron felt his anger die away as he stared into the chairwoman's eyes, and eventually he nodded. "Thank you, Madam Chairwoman."

The Chairwoman smiled again at Theron. "Please, you're the son of two people I used to work closely with, and I hope you and I will also be able to work together in the future. It feels a bit strange to have you address me so stiffly. Call me Uma."

Theron's eyes widened in shock. He remembered

how everyone else he'd talked with referred to her. *The chairwoman is allowing someone like me to call her by name? Given how everyone else addresses her, she must be giving me a great privilege. I wonder what this feeling is. Is this what it means to feel special? This kind of warm, uplifting feeling? I don't know how to respond to it. Would I have been able to feel this way more often if my parents hadn't died? Would I be more accustomed to such positive feelings?* As he was musing, he heard a knock on the door.

Uma sighed, then stood and looked towards the door. "Enter."

The door opened and Deacon walked in. He repeated the same three steps followed by a bow that he had performed the first time he had entered. "Everything is ready for the meeting Madam Chairwoman."

Uma nodded. "Very well. Theron, I hope I will have an opportunity to speak to you again soon, but for now I'll have to send you to your dormitory. The dorm mother should already be aware of your arrival. She'll be able to direct you to your room."

"Oh, I need to stop by the female dorm first. A friend there asked me to tell her about how this meeting went." Theron remembered his promise to Katerina.

"So you already made a friend?" Uma smiled. "I suppose that's not all that surprising. Well, it should be fine, just don't stay out too late."

"I won't," Theron assured Uma as he got up from his chair and began walking out of the room.

"I'll see you soon," Deacon told Theron as he walked past. As Theron turned to close the doors on his way out, he noticed the chairwoman on the phone, already back at work. Theron once again marveled at his encounter with Uma. He understood why everyone seemed to talk about her with a sense of awe.

Theron entered the elevator and pressed the button for the ground floor. He pulled his admission papers out from his pocket and flipped to the campus map as he rode the elevator down. He traced the route he'd need to take to get to the female dormitory from the high school. He then put the papers back in his pocket as he felt the elevator slow as it neared the bottom floor. Theron got off the elevator and headed towards the building exit on the far side of the locker room.

When Theron left the building he noticed it had gotten much darker down on the campus grounds, dark enough to call it night instead of late evening, with the moon shining down. He turned to his left as he stepped onto the walkway encircling the high school and began traveling counter clockwise. He took the first path on his right. It would lead directly to the female dorm if he ignored all the intersecting walkways. The paths were lit with a combination of glowing green phosphorescent lamps spaced out a meter apart and large solar lamps spaced ten meters apart.

As he walked down the path, he began to hear a voice. It sounded like it was yelling out, but Theron couldn't make out any words. He decided to follow the sound of the voice, and picked up his pace to a jog as he listened. He jogged for about two hundred meters before he could make out the shouting and realized they were cries for help. Now Theron started running. He was a great athlete, and he covered the remaining distance to the voice, about another hundred meters, in about ten seconds. He had crossed into a baseball field which obviously hadn't had any field maintenance while the students were away. There he saw a scene brought him to a dead stop.

For the third time that day, Theron found himself captivated by a beautiful girl, but this time the beauty of the woman was juxtaposed with a scene from a horror movie. The woman was easily the equal of the chairwoman in beauty, but her eyes, rather than the red-violet of the chairwoman's, were a deep true violet, and they seemed to glow in the night. She was tall, probably close to a hundred eighty centimeters. She was wearing a suit of black leather armor, which, even though it seemed anachronistic, somehow enhanced the woman's attractiveness. Her long hair shone like polished silver in the moonlight. Theron also noticed a silver bracelet gleaming on the pale, translucent skin of the woman's relaxed left arm. The very sight of her would be enough to make someone forget to breathe.

In her right hand the woman held a boy wearing beige slacks and a green polo shirt. Despite the casual clothes, the boy had to be a high school student. He was still letting out strangled screams for help. The screams weren't nearly as loud as before. The woman's right hand tightened around the boy's throat. It was clear this woman was choking the life out of the student, lifting him nearly a foot off the ground with the one hand gripping his neck.

What happened next made the hairs on the back of Theron's neck stand on end. A pale green light had started seeping out and rising from the pores in the boy's skin. It started to take the shape of a human. The face of the form showed it felt unbearable pain. The light began to slowly stretch out from the form's chest and coil around the woman's arm, blending in to her skin as if it were being drawn into her. As more light moved towards the woman, Theron noticed his ears could no longer hear the boy's screams, but he could still feel them. He realized he was hearing the soundless screams of the boy's soul as it was being ripped from its now limp physical body.

Theron's own body couldn't move as he watched the last of the light leave the boy and be absorbed by the woman. Then the boy's body was tossed aside like trash. With the gruesome scene finished in front of him, Theron found he could move again, but the sudden change in his body's behavior made him fall before he could catch himself. The motion caught the woman's attention and she turned towards Theron.

"Tsk, it seems I've been seen by an innocent." The woman advanced towards Theron. It looked like she was moving so slowly, but the amount of time she took to cover the distance between them was far too short. Theron didn't even have time to get up. He could only backpedal on all fours as he tried futilely to get away. "I guess you've seen too much, but don't worry. I won't kill you. I'll only play with your memories for a bit."

Theron thought he saw a tendril extend out from the woman's hand and reach towards him, but he realized he was feeling it approach, not actually seeing it with his eyes. The tendril brushed up against his forehead, and he started to feel pressure build up in his mind. He gripped his head in both hands and tried to fight back against the pressure. He had no idea what was going on anymore. He could only see the beautiful woman in front of him as he felt waves of dizziness wash over him. Then he couldn't see or feel anything.

Chapter 2

A Dangerous Game

The first thing Theron noticed was a low humming sound. It sounded muffled, like it was a long way off, but slowly, as he focused on the sound, it seemed to draw closer, sounding almost like the buzzing of an insect. Theron tried to brush the sound away, but he found his arm wouldn't obey his thoughts. Then he noticed a pleasant smell fill his nose, like a freshly bloomed flower garden, and he began to see a red haze. It slowly dawned on him that his eyes were closed, and the red he was seeing must be sunlight directly hitting his eye lids.

Theron noticed a weight on his left side. He tried to move his right arm again, it felt heavy, but at least this time it responded. He used his hand to shield his closed eyes from the sun, and slowly forced his eyelids to open. Things were blurry at first, but finally started coming into focus. Theron realized the buzzing sound he heard was a heater. He saw white curtains that could be drawn to make a partition. He noticed a glass cabinet with a lock on it with pill bottles, gauze, and other medical equipment inside. He guessed he was in a hospital or clinic of some kind.

As his eyes continued to slowly shift around the

room, his gaze finally came down to rest on the weight he felt on his side. He could see Katerina's rich red hair spread out beside him. Her head gently rested on him. Apparently she had fallen asleep at his bedside. Without thinking, he moved his left hand and softly stroked her hair. Katerina stirred as she felt the pressure. When she realized someone was touching her she sat bolt upright and looked around. Seeing no one else, she realized Theron had been the one stroking her hair.

"You're finally awake! Thank heavens. No matter how much I tried to wake you up you wouldn't open your eyes. I was so worried about you!" Katerina seemed like she was holding back tears.

"What am I doing here? Why is it so bright?" Theron managed to ask in a hoarse voice.

Katerina noticed Theron was still shielding his eyes from the sunlight, so she got up and drew the blinds over the window. Then she looked at the clock, confirming the time. "You've been unconscious for over eighteen hours now. I was starting to get worried about you yesterday evening. It seemed like your meeting was lasting a really long time, and it was already pretty dark out, so I had decided to go to the high school and wait for you to finish so I could talk to you, rather than make you come all the way to the female dorms. As I was walking I noticed two people lying on the baseball field, so I went over to check on them."

At this point Katerina seemed to be talking mechanically, trying to list off the order things happened in without actually revisiting the memory. She was just staring off into space as she began reciting what happened. "The first boy was a middle school student. I knew there was no way he had just fallen asleep. His body position was too unnatural, more fitting a corpse, really. He was still breathing, but I knew something was horribly wrong. I remembered last term there were rumors of students just being found in random places that had fallen into comas, never to wake up. I knew there wasn't anything I could do for him, so I turned to the next boy, and I could feel my heart stop."

She couldn't hold back her emotions as the memory gripped her. Tears started running silently down her cheeks and she looked directly at Theron. "I recognized it was you. I was so terrified that you would be like the other boy, unable to wake. I called out to you. I shook you. I tried everything I could think of but you weren't waking up. I was so scared. I ran as hard as I could to the medical facility. I got a nurse to come back with me to try to wake you up, but even the smelling salt she tried wouldn't work. I had this terrible sinking feeling in my heart. You could have been lost to this world because of me. Because I made you promise to come and see me!"

Katerina was almost in hysterics at this point. Theron forced himself out of bed and held her, trying to calm her down. At first she tried to push back, afraid he would blame her for what happened, but he continued to hold her close. "It's not your fault. To be honest, I was happy about all the attention you gave me yesterday. I was surprised that you asked me to meet you last night, but I wasn't displeased. I made that promise because I wanted to see you, not because you forced me into it."

Hearing his words, Katerina stopped struggling and seemed to slump into him, letting his arms support her. "Really? I'm not just causing trouble for you?"

"I don't think you cause me any trouble. Besides, you stayed by my side all this time didn't you? I don't know why you care for me so much, but you certainly aren't a burden," Theron answered to comfort her, but in his mind he felt that he couldn't understand her. *Why does she care for me so much? She just met me yesterday.* Again though, now wasn't the time to ask her. Besides, hearing Katerina's story made him remember what he had seen last night. That woman was definitely somewhere on campus. *I know she'll come seek me out again, but who would believe me if I tried to explain what happened and ask for help? What could I say? That a beautiful woman was sucking out people's souls?* There was nothing he could do about it at the moment, but maybe he could still request protection from the chairwoman. He'd have to come up with an excuse for it.

Suddenly Theron heard a gurgling sound, and he felt Katerina tighten up. "Um, I haven't eaten anything since dinner yesterday," she said, sounding embarrassed.

Theron released Katerina and stepped back, looking at her with a grin. "I haven't either. Come to think of it, I heard the dining hall is in the same area as the medical facility. Care to lead me to the cafeteria?"

Katerina finally smiled and nodded. "Sure, just let me call the nurse first and let her know you woke up and that I'll be taking you to get something to eat." She walked over to a desk and picked up the phone sitting on it. She hit a speed dial button. After a few seconds she began telling the nurse that Theron was awake and seemed to be fine. She gave a few affirmations over the phone, then hung up.

"So, what did the nurse say?" Theron asked.

"She said it was okay to take you to the dining hall, but after we're done eating we need to come back so she can run a few tests to make sure you're okay," Katerina answered.

"That sounds reasonable. Well then, lead on. I didn't even get dinner yesterday," Theron reminded her with a smile.

"Of course!" Katerina said happily as she walked towards the door.

Theron followed her out the door and down a hallway. It appeared there were several rooms in the medical facility, each one overseen by a different nurse. When they reached the end of a hallway they came to a sliding glass door. There was a hiss signifying a pressure exchange. It seemed the medical wing was air tight, probably in case it was necessary to quarantine someone. Theron stepped out of the medical facility into another hallway. On his left was a door leading to the outside. On the right, there was a staircase leading to the upper floors. He saw a sign on the wall near the steps that explained that art, music, and design rooms were on the second and third floors.

Directly in front of him was another sliding glass door that led to the dining hall. It was a large room, probably thirty by twenty-five meters, filled with enough chairs and tables to seat over five hundred people. There were close to a hundred people in the room already eating when Katerina and Theron entered the dining hall.

Katerina lead the way to a long table with numerous kinds of food on display. "For today we'll have to settle for the buffet. If you ever want a specific meal prepared you have to order it in advance so it can be prepared, but the chefs we have here are world class, and even the items on the buffet are wonderful."

"I'll keep that in mind," Theron said as he picked up a plate and began selecting various kinds of food. Once he had filled his plate, he waited for Katerina to finish getting her food and together they walked over to an empty table and sat down. It wasn't long after they started eating that Theron noticed Deacon enter the dining hall. Deacon started looking around. He spotted

Theron and came over to the table.

"Hey Theron! I heard you woke up. That's a relief. The chairwoman asked me to let you know that she wants to see you. Please go see her as soon as you're able. I have a one-time pass keycard for you to go up and talk to her. The nurse who was looking after you is already aware, and has agreed to wait till after your meeting to complete your examination." Deacon handed a card over to Theron. "Also, I found out from the dorm mother in the male dormitory that you didn't have any clothes delivered, and I guess you don't have any school uniforms yet, so when you come back for your exam you can also go upstairs to one of the design rooms. You'll be directed to people who can help make sure new clothes are fitted for you."

Deacon next looked over at Katerina. "Good day to you, Miss Aikia. I heard you stayed with Theron the whole time he was unconscious. Thanks for looking after him."

"It's not something you need to thank me for, Mr. President." Katerina gave Deacon a tight, empty smile. It was nothing like any of the smiles she had shown Theron.

"Well, I don't want to interrupt your meal, and that's all I had." Deacon turned and took a few steps before stopping and turning back towards the table. "Oh, wait. There was one more thing. Tomorrow we're having our opening ceremony and class assignments. I know I already told you what class you're in, but I want to make sure you attend the ceremony. As the special scholarship student for this term, you'll be formally introduced to the student body. It'll also be a good chance to meet the other members of the Student Council."

"Okay, I'll be there." Theron nodded at Deacon before watching the president leave the dining hall.

Katerina cleared her throat to get Theron's attention. "So, you've already met the president, and you even know what class you'll be in. Since you didn't get to tell me what happened at your meeting yesterday, maybe you can tell me now." There was a hint of displeasure in Katerina's voice. For some reason, Theron didn't think the tone was actually directed towards him, but at the idea that other people had also gotten to know him when she wasn't there. Maybe she was the jealous and possessive type.

"Yeah, he had to escort me up to the chairwoman's office because I didn't have a keycard, and he also took the opportunity to give me a tour of the high school. During the tour he told me I'd be in Class 2-B until they can observe my social interaction skills," Theron explained.

"Class 2-B?" Katerina's eyes lit up. "That's probably the class I'll be in as well, but I suppose you'll be moving up to Class A shortly. Maybe you could help me study? My grades have been holding me back from reaching Class A, but if you're going to move up soon, I'll have to try harder so I can keep up with you."

Theron frowned. "I don't mind helping you study of course, but I have to ask: why are you so interested in me? I noticed the way you talked to Deacon. At first I thought that maybe you were just nice to everyone, but it's becoming apparent that I'm something special to you. Could you please tell me why?" Theron had finally asked the question that had been lingering in his mind throughout all the time he had spent the Katerina. He hoped it wasn't too soon. He didn't want to push her away, but he had been taken advantage of too much to just blindly trust her.

Katerina's fork froze in place and she began biting her lip. "I've been telling myself the same thing, you know. It's silly, I know, but I can't seem to help it. Ever since I saw you on the train yesterday, I've been feeling drawn to you. I've only felt this way once before. There was a boy I used to play with when I was much younger. I would hang out with him at parties. I don't remember very well, but I recall he was sickly. Though later on, when I started visiting his house, he seemed much stronger. Then suddenly my family stopped visiting that boy's house. I remember my parents seemed sad about it too. They told me that the boy didn't want to see us anymore."

Katerina shook her head, trying to shake away the memory. "Anyway, I've never felt so attached to anyone else, and I was shocked when I felt such a strong connection to you when I saw you. I know it makes no sense. I've been telling myself you're not the boy I knew, but when I saw you last night, and thought that I might lose you too, I realized it didn't matter. I believe I'm being given a second chance at being a part of the life of someone with such a large presence in my heart. Please don't hate me for being so weird. If you need me to take a step back, I will, but please don't push me out of your life."

Theron was silent as he thought about her story. Something about it caused a faint tickle in the back of his mind, but he couldn't quite grasp hold of what it was. Still, it was enough to understand. For some reason, Theron had also felt a stronger connection to Katerina than he had to other girls he'd known. He wouldn't be able to explain it if pressed. It wasn't quite love. He didn't believe in love at first sight, but he did believe that sometimes the connections between people were a matter of fate, that it was inevitable. He wouldn't say he loved her, just as she hadn't said she loved him, but he would agree with Katerina's description of being a large presence in his heart. He realized he didn't want to let her go either.

The realization that they actually felt the same way brought a sense of peace to Theron. Their experiences were just different. Where Theron had been betrayed by people he should have been able to trust, and therefore treated people with suspicion and pushed them away, Katerina had lost someone important to her. Now that she had more power to actively affect the events in her life, she wanted to make sure she didn't lose someone again. It was simple enough.

"I won't push you away. I'd be honored to be your friend," Theron told Katerina.

Katerina's head had dropped down low while Theron had thought through everything, but when she heard his response it came back up, her eyes opened wide. "Really? You don't think I'm too weird?"

"I don't really think it's appropriate to tease or lie in a situation like this, so yes, really. You may be a bit weird, but it just so happens I don't mind weird people," Theron said with a bit of a grin. "Anyway, we'd better finish eating. Apparently my schedule got filled up while I was unconscious."

Katerina nodded. "Yeah, I need to get everything ready for my classes since there won't be much time tomorrow with all the opening ceremony and orientation stuff."

The two finished eating. They parted ways without saying much else, just enjoying one another's company. Theron felt much more relaxed around Katerina now, and this time as they parted they both turned back to look at each other several times, smiling each time.

Theron continued on to the high school building and went straight to the elevators. This time he noticed other students in the building. He remembered the teacher yesterday telling him that the classroom tours for new students were today, so he guessed all the students were mostly first years. He called the elevator and stepped on once the door opened. He pressed the button for the top floor and used the keycard he had been given. Once he reached the top, he knocked on the door.

Instead of hearing the chairwoman call for him this time, Deacon opened the door for him and gestured him in. "Welcome, I'm glad you could make it."

"I wouldn't turn down the chairwoman," Theron told Deacon. He walked in and approached Uma's desk. "May I sit down, Madam Chairwoman?"

"Of course, you don't even need to ask, and remember what I told you yesterday." The chairwoman smiled at him.

Theron sat down in one of the chairs across from the desk. He still wasn't comfortable with just plopping down, but he wasn't as conscientious about being formal either. "So, I assume you want to talk with me about what happened after I left last night Uma?"

Theron heard a strangled noise behind him as Deacon approached. Uma ignored the sound and nodded. "Yes. The other boy found at the scene still hasn't woken up, and unlike your situation, he registered no higher brain functions. His heart is beating and he's breathing, but he'll never wake up. He's basically an empty shell."

The chairwoman sighed and rubbed her temples. "This is not the first time this has happened. Eight other students have been found in similar condition over the past year. No one has been able to make anything of it, but this is the first time someone else has been found at the scene. So I have to ask, can you remember what happened?"

Theron hesitated. The more he ran the events through his mind, the more absurd they seemed. *How can I tell her I saw a person that can pull a person's soul out of his body and absorb it? And what about what the woman did to me before I blacked out? She said she was going to play with my memories. What if she succeeded? What if what I remember isn't what really happened? Or if the events themselves are real, and someone actually does have the power to rip out a person's soul, how else might my memories have changed? What if my memory of the person who committed the crime was what got altered? What if I end up falsely accusing someone?*

Seeing his hesitation, the chairwoman came around to him, much as she had yesterday. "Theron, I know this might seem like an absurd question, but do you believe in the existence of the soul? You see, there is nothing physically wrong with any of the victims. There is no scientific explanation for what has happened to them. Personally, I believe it's possible something has happened to their souls."

The statement finally made Theron nod. At least the chairwoman probably wouldn't doubt him. He explained everything that he saw last night to the chairwoman. He also expressed his concerns about the possibility that his memory had been tampered with.

After hearing his story, Uma patted Theron's hand. "I don't think you have to worry about your memories being altered. I believe the attacker failed in her attempts to do that. The fact that you were able to feel her intrusion into your mind and fight it off is significant in that regard. Still, I had some crazy suspicions about what was going on, but I never thought they'd be confirmed."

"What do you mean?" Theron asked her.

Uma hesitated before continuing. "There are ancient myths about beings with the powers you described. Some of these myths date back over four millennia. I had half believed myself crazy for considering it, but no other solution seemed to fit. I believe the person you saw is a psychic vampire: a being capable of absorbing life energy directly from another person's body. Because they can directly intervene in the natural flow of a person's energy, they can also have a strong influence over the electrochemical impulses in the brain, thus the ability to alter memories. However, according to my research, it's possible for just about anyone to learn to control their own personal energy, so it's possible that through instinct and desperation, and perhaps a good deal of raw natural talent, you were able to fight off her psychic attack."

Theron was shocked. Instead of the doubt he had expected, he had been validated by the chairwoman and given a name to put to the things he had witnessed. "What should we do about this?" Theron asked.

Uma sighed again. "There isn't really anything we can do against the vampire yet. Even if you and I know the truth, how do we prove it? No one will believe us with our words alone. Anyway, our first priority should be to protect you. It's possible you'll meet the psychic vampire again on the campus. If you recognize her, try not to let on that you know what she is. Try to act as if her memory alteration worked and you've never seen her before. Your first line of defense is making her think she succeeded in whatever she tried to do to you.

"I think there's also a possibility you may be the best one to fight against her. After all, your will was strong enough to defend against her attack, maybe with training you would be able to go on the offensive. As I mentioned before, I've done some research on the matter, mostly studying eastern meditation techniques. I'll do what I can to teach you how to control your own energy. With some luck, we'll be able to figure out how to use that control against this monster."

Theron nodded. "I'll try my best."

"To that end, I'm going to give you this keycard. This isn't a one-time pass like the one you were given earlier. With this you can come see me any time. President Cynan, please escort Theron out. Then return to me. We need to discuss some plans for campus security," the chairwoman commanded. Deacon bowed, accepting the orders.

Theron took the card from Uma and started walking towards the elevator with Deacon. Before they got on, Deacon spoke to him. "You got pretty close with the chairwoman last night I take it? I've never met anyone she allowed to call her freely by name like that."

"Apparently she was a friend of my parents. She asked me to call her Uma," Theron responded.

"I see. For an orphan, you have a lot of connections," Deacon commented, sounding almost snide. Theron guessed he was jealous, given that Deacon had been working closely with the chairwoman for a while now as Student Council President.

"I knew my parents were well liked by a lot of people, but I never expected anything like this. Things are really moving a bit too fast for me. I'm really sorry if I'm stepping on your toes," Theron apologized.

Deacon realized that he had crossed a line and grinned at Theron. "I guess I'm the one that should apologize, it's not your fault, after all. Our positions are just that different. Anyway, I'll see you tomorrow at the opening ceremony."

"Yeah, I'll see you there," Theron answered as he got on the elevator. He saw Deacon waving at him as the door closed. Theron's next stop was to go back to the nurses office. It only took him a few minutes to get back to the room he had woken up in earlier. This time the nurse was present.

"This will only take a few moments. I just need to perform a few tests. Please sit down and look straight ahead." After Theron sat down, the nurse started shining a light in Theron's eye. He strained as hard as he could not to blink. The light blinded him to the point that he couldn't really see what was going on even after the light source was removed, but he felt a reflex hammer striking his knee next. Then the nurse wrapped a band around his arm and started checking his blood pressure. Soon enough, his vision cleared and he saw the nurse writing her report.

"Is everything all right?" Theron asked.

"Well, your eyes seem very photosensitive," the nurse answered.

"That's a preexisting condition. My eyes have always been sensitive to bright lights, and they don't fully adjust to them," Theron explained.

"I see. Well, if that's the case, then everything else checks out." The nurse made some notations on a piece of paper. "You're free to go, but please come back if you feel anything wrong, even mild disorientation and dizziness."

"I will," Theron affirmed before leaving the nurses office.

Next he went up to the second floor and looked for the design rooms. He saw another student and called out. "Excuse me, could you help me find a room where I can get some new clothes fitted?"

"Oh, you must be Theron. We've been expecting you. Please come this way." The boy guided Theron to a room filled with clothes and fabrics. There were numerous male uniforms on display as well. Most of the uniforms were matched with khaki slacks, but some had dark colored slacks ranging from navy blue to black. Some uniforms had a short sleeve shirt matched with a sweater vest. Other uniforms had a white long sleeve shirt matched with a blazer and tie. There were several colors of blazers and ties to choose form. It was clear that color choice was the easiest way for a person to personalize their clothes, while the actual style of clothes was fairly limited.

"I've found him," the student said to the other people already inside.

An older male student greeted him. "Ah good, we've been waiting for you. I'm the Tailoring Club President. I understand you need a whole wardrobe, including school uniforms."

"Yes, and I'm sorry for the trouble." Theron bowed his head in apology.

"Oh, no need to worry about it. After all, we're all here because we love working on clothes. Besides, the academy is even paying us a bonus," the club president answered.

"I had no idea." Theron guessed either Deacon or the chairwoman had made the arrangements. He would have to thank them once again later.

"Okay, first we need to take your measurements. We can just adjust the school uniforms and have them sent to your room tonight so you'll have them for tomorrow, but casual clothes will take some time because they'll be custom made." Another student, this time a female, came up to him with a tape measure.

"Oh, that's all right. As long as I have my school uniforms, I'm in no rush for the rest." Theron felt a bit overwhelmed as his body was repositioned by the three students he'd been talking to and his measurements were taken. It seemed like it was over in a flash as the girl wrote down all the numbers on a piece of paper.

"All right, we've got everything we need. Is there any particular style you like?" the club president asked. "You'll get all the uniform types of course, but we'd like to know your preferences for colors and the casual clothes."

Theron thought for a moment before answering. "I

don't really have much experience with fashion. I suppose a combination of formal attire and things that are comfortable and easy to move in? Maybe just a few outfits at first, then I'll be able to give you some feedback and we can figure out more of what I like from there? As for colors, I like darker shades, so I guess black, dark blue, dark green, and things like that. I do like crimson as well."

Another one of the club members laughed. "You should really be more careful about giving a designer relatively free rein like that, but I guess it'll do for now."

Theron felt a bit apprehensive hearing that, but there wasn't anything else he could do. Suddenly there was a knock on the open door behind him. Theron turned around and froze. In front of him was the woman he had seen the night before. At least he thought it was. The hair color was a bit different. Instead of polished silver, it was a beautiful platinum blonde color that could reflect any light it caught in its tresses. Her eyes also weren't a glowing true violet like they were the previous night. Her eyes were currently a very deep shade of blue, but they still held hints of the violet color he remembered. However, what really convinced Theron that this was the same woman that attacked the student was the silver bracelet on her forearm. For some reason it stood out clearly in his memory. This time he noticed that she actually wore one on each arm. Theron quickly tried to cover up his shock as he remembered the chairwoman's caution to pretend like he'd never seen this woman before.

"I'm here to check on one of my patients. My nurse informed me he checked out okay, but I just wanted to verify his condition." The woman's eyes had focused on Theron as she spoke.

"Oh, Doctor Vaashti, we just finished with him, so

he's all yours," the club president told her.

"That's wonderful. Please follow me Mr. Zeyla," the doctor requested in a kind tone that caught Theron a little by surprise. Even knowing what this woman was, he still couldn't deny a strong attraction to her. He felt his legs moving after her even though he didn't consciously tell them to do so.

"So, you're the doctor on campus?" Theron dared to ask.

"Yes, my name is Trish Vaashti. You may address me as Doctor Vaashti," the woman responded.

When they were alone in the hallway, she turned and looked deep into Theron's eyes. He tried not to tremble and instead forced his head to tilt as if he were curious about what she was doing. "Is something wrong?"

"What are you?" Trish asked.

The question caught Theron completely off guard. "What do you mean? I'm a transfer student here."

Trish pursed her lips before answering in a louder voice, one that could be heard in the room they'd just left, but not so loud as to sound unnatural. "I'm really concerned about the findings the nurse had. People don't just fall into a coma for no reason and then wake up eighteen hours later as if nothing happened. I'm going to need to keep you under observation until I can get to the bottom of this. I'm going to be recommending you for health officer duty since I'll be expecting to see you every day anyway. We can kill two birds with one stone that way."

Theron knew he was in trouble. He was going to have to spend every day with this murderess? But what could he say to stop it? He would have to tell the chairwoman about this as soon as possible.

Apparently Trish took his silence for acceptance. "Well, I'll be expecting to see you after the orientation following the opening ceremony tomorrow."

Theron couldn't argue at this point. He couldn't refute the doctor's claims that he needed to be under observation without revealing that he knew what happened the previous night. Trish, seeming satisfied, turned and walked away down the stairs.

As soon as he felt it was safe, Theron took off back to the high school building. He passed several students, but he was running too fast to really take notice of them. He managed to slow himself down before he crashed into the entrance of the high school. He yanked the door open and power walked to the elevator, pressing the button. The door opened and he got in, pressed the button for the top floor, and used his new keycard. The elevator began its ascent. The minute of standing still as he waited for it to reach the top felt like forever.

When he finally reached the door he barely stopped himself from bursting in. He calmed his nerves as much as he could and knocked, but before his fist could land the door opened. Uma was standing there looking worried.

"What's wrong Theron? You look awful," the chairwoman asked him with a voice full of concern.

"The woman, I saw last night, was the school's doctor," Theron started to explain haltingly between breaths. He was still breathing fairly hard from his exertion and fright, "She said she was going to have me come to her for observation every day."

Uma put her hands on Theron's shoulders and made him look her in the eyes. A feeling of calm immediately began to take hold as he gazed into her eyes. "It'll be all right Theron. Unfortunately, if the doctor is the woman you saw last night, there isn't much we can do in this situation yet. We need evidence to act against her. You'll have to play along with her for now, but on the positive side, you've passed the hard part. Now that you really do know her, you don't have to pretend as hard. Just don't let on that you know what she did, and you'll be fine. After a few weeks of observation, President Cynan or I will intervene, saying she has no medical reason to keep you under such a close watch. At that time, I'd like you to join the Student Council. Nothing else in our plans has changed. Starting in two days, when normal classes start, report to me every day after you meet with the doctor and we'll start your lessons in energy control."

Theron nodded. If he had bothered to think things through he would have realized all this on his own. He felt a little embarrassed for bothering the chairwoman like this.

"You're thinking you shouldn't have bothered me, aren't you?" Uma half asked and half stated. "You did the right thing. Even if nothing has changed, you were still right in reporting the situation to me. We're partners in this now. I want you to come to me with everything," Uma told Theron to help comfort him. "Now, you still haven't reported to your dorm mother have you? Go do that, and try to relax for the rest of the day."

"All right." Theron nodded then turned to leave. When he got on the elevator and turned back toward the chairwoman's office, he saw Uma smiling at him and nodding in encouragement before the doors closed to take him back down to the first floor. Theron began to wonder how he had become so dependent on someone else, especially after what he had been through at the orphanage. Maybe it was because Uma reminded him a bit of his mother. She was so kind and confidant. It was hard not to rely on her, but, somewhere in the back of his mind, he felt a sense of discomfort in trusting her. For now, he pushed the feeling down by thinking Uma wasn't like the other adults that had betrayed him, but the feeling wouldn't fully go away.

He left the high school with his feet dragging a bit. Again there were other students on the path, but he was too lost in his own inner turmoil to notice them. He was so lost in his thoughts that he was surprised when he arrived at the male dormitory. He walked into the building and went to the reception desk to speak with the dorm mother.

"I'm Theron Zeyla, here to check in," Theron said. He still wasn't able to force any cheer into his voice.

"Ah, we've been waiting for you. My name is Ms. Norris. I've been informed that you've had a rough first day, so I'm sure you're eager to be able to relax a bit. Your room number is sixty-four. Here are your keycards." The dorm mother handed him five key cards.

"Why so many?" Theron asked.

"They're all labeled. You have your room key and a duplicate. There's a key to the building in case you need to stay out after closing hours, a key to the laundry room, and a key to the computer lab. We have exercise rooms and a communal bath. Of course, each room has its own bathroom, but the large hot spring in the communal area is quite popular. Also, take this." The dorm mother handed Theron a small booklet. "This is a phone directory for the campus. Some numbers require special passcodes to go through, like the chairwoman's. After all, it wouldn't do to have her phone ringing off its hook all the time."

Theron quickly flipped through the booklet. "There's even a number for a masseuse?"

The dorm mother looked amused. "Yes, though I imagine that's mostly used by the girls, the booklet is general issue after all. Still, you all are elite children, so even if the classes are strict, here in the dorms we tend to be a bit extravagant."

"Well, I doubt I'll be too demanding, just having my own room feels extravagant," Theron commented. "So, which way is my room?"

"Rooms fifty-one through one hundred are on your right. You'll find signs posted along the way indicating where the various amenities are. Feel free to go exploring or mingle with your neighbors. We don't actually impose a curfew, but we do lock the doors into the building at twenty-one hundred hours and ask that tenants keep noise to a minimum after that time. Do remember we also have elementary students housed here, so I ask that all older residents set a good example and help them when they can."

"I have some experience with that. Anyway, thank you for your help." Theron nodded his head gratefully towards Ms. Norris before he turned to his right and walked down the hallway. It didn't take long to reach the door marked sixty-four. He used the keycard and opened the door.

Inside was a large writing desk with copies of all the text books he'd need for class stacked on top. There was also a full size bed with a nightstand on each side. One stand had an alarm clock. The other stand had a phone on it. He walked over to the stand with the phone and put the booklet he had received beside it. He noticed on the phone there was a direct dial number he could share with others so they wouldn't have to go through the dorm reception desk. He made a mental note to share his number with Katerina, and try to get her number too.

There was no TV, not that it could get reception even if there were. He went into the bathroom. It appeared spacious, with a full size bathtub and plenty of counter space. There was a walk-in closet that could be entered from either the bathroom or the bedroom. Taken altogether, the room was a king's suite compared to what he was used to.

Theron threw himself onto the bed, feeling it out. He found a controller underneath the right hand pillow that let him adjust the firmness of the mattress, but he didn't have any experience with different firmness levels, so he decided to leave it alone for the time being. If he found it caused him to be stiff or sore he could try adjusting it later. As he lay on the bed, he noticed how exhausted he felt. It seemed passing out like he had last night wasn't the same as normal sleep, so now his body was starting to crave rest. He'd probably wake up in a few hours, hopefully in time to receive his clothes, and maybe he'd try to get hold of Katerina before she could go to sleep. His thoughts began to slip as he got drowsier. Finally he gave up on thinking and let sleep take him.

* * * * *

Trish Vaashti sat at her computer in her office. She had been trying to perform a background check on Theron Zeyla for almost an hour now, but so far she wasn't able to find out anything. She'd have to ask him where he came from or what hospital he used to go to when he was sick so she could request medical records. She didn't even know what country's databases to check to start finding other background information. She could go to look at the student records in the administration building, but she wasn't sure she could trust them. Someone high up in the school administration, either in the Student Council or among the senior faculty, was an enemy. That was the only way to explain the kind of access her quarry seemed to have. Trish tried to organize her thoughts, going over the events she had experienced since the first encounter with Theron.

I didn't know it was possible, Trish thought to herself, *but somehow that boy Theron fended off my attempts to wipe his memory. I knew I felt his resistance last night.* Because of that feeling she had decided to check in on him while he was unconscious. *I would have known for sure earlier if that girl, I believe she said her name was Katerina, hadn't been there. Now I have another mystery piled on top of the problems I'm already facing.*

With that girl there Trish hadn't been able to perform any probes, but she had noticed something that should be impossible. A small amount of energy was being drawn out of the girl and drifting into an unconscious Theron. When Trish saw that she left as quickly as she could without arousing the girl's suspicions and instructed the nurse to let her know if the girl started feeling anything, passing it off as concern that she might catch whatever had caused Theron to fall into his comatose state.

Trish knew people could learn to consciously control energy. She even knew a special few could absorb energy from others, but to do so while unconscious was another matter altogether. Perhaps it was the girl giving her energy to the boy. Intense emotion and focus could allow for small energy transfers, though to keep up such a steady stream would be highly unusual. When the nurse had come to her thirty minutes later telling her that Katerina had seemed to get fatigued unusually quickly and had fallen asleep, Trish had gone back and confirmed that energy was indeed still being passed from the sleeping girl to the unconscious boy.

She had attempted to cut the flow with her own abilities, but the connection was too strong. The bond between the two was too deep to be cut without their desiring it. Trish didn't know what kind of bond those two shared, but it made her uncomfortable. In the nearly two hundred years Trish had been alive, she had never been that close to anyone. To be honest, she felt a little jealous, but what was the point of forming those connections when everyone else she met would be dead long before her?

She put those musings aside and refocused her thoughts, running through the last few hours in her mind again. After she had learned Theron had woken up, she had gone to find him. As soon as he saw her, she knew her suspicions that she had failed to clear his memory were correct. His body had frozen and his eyes widened slightly, but he had covered it up quickly.

Someone had to have coached him to play along. She had spent some time trying to find out whom all he had spoken to, but not many other students recognized him yet, so it was hard to retrace his steps. All she learned was that the Student Council President spoke to a boy no one knew in the dining hall. The only thing that came out of her questioning was that she had more reason to be suspicious of the Student Council than before. She had thought to speak to the girl, Katerina, but it was obvious the girl was too close to Theron. Trish didn't want him to know how much she was investigating him. Theron had started a dangerous game with her by trying to pretend he didn't recognize her. Now she had to play along, so she couldn't officially express an interest in him beyond a professional level.

Sometimes she really hated the rules her kind had to operate by. It was absolutely forbidden to kill an innocent human. If there was even the possibility that a person wasn't actually involved, she couldn't harm them. She required absolute confirmation. This academy was a nest for sanguine vampires, or sangs for short. The sangs were beings that sucked the lifeblood out of their victims and killed them, but Trish had never seen sangs behave as the ones here did. Usually they would just feed on and kill their prey, but these seemed more interested in spreading their numbers than simply feeding. They had even started being more cautious about their activities when her presence was known.

She had loved the concept behind this academy when she first heard of it. Her job was the guardianship of humanity after all, so seeing humans come together to get to know one another to ensure peace in the future was a truly uplifting sight. However, it was also a major point of vulnerability. Given that the sangs' overall objective was the destruction of human civilization, this gathering of the future hope of the world was too tempting to ignore.

Thus, Trish had come to this school just in case something happened, and found that the sangs were already spreading like a cancer. Their level of organization indicated that a very powerful vampire was behind everything. Maybe even a primogen, one of the first generation sanguine vampires. If that was the case, would she be up to the task of killing them all?

Trish didn't know, but there was no point worrying about it now. The question before her was what to do about Theron Zeyla. *Given his reaction and the recent activities of the sanguine vampires, it seems likely that last night was a setup. The vampire I killed was sent as an intentional play meant to draw me to a place where my actions would be witnessed by that boy. That means they wanted Theron to see me kill someone. Why?*

The question led Trish to a few conclusions. *I suppose that Theron didn't know about vampires, sanguine or psychic, before last night. The sangs must have wanted to make him aware. They probably also wanted to make him an ally in fighting against me, which means that, at least for the moment, he isn't on their side. Still, why go through the trouble of orchestrating that little show all for his benefit? He's clearly not normal given the fact that he can absorb energy from other people subconsciously, as if he were a...* At that point Trish's thoughts trailed off. She had an answer, but it was impossible.

It can't be, there are only six psychic vampires in the world. How could this be possible? We're even forbidden from having children because they won't be born as one of us. Still, the evidence suggested that Theron was one of them. Trish slumped in her chair. *If it is true, then that means an untrained, inexperience monster just got thrust on my lap. What a mess.* Trish sighed. *But if I don't try to reach out and teach him, the sangs will. They must have realized what he is, which is why they want him on their side.* Trish sighed again as she rested her forehead on her hand. *I'm still too young to raise a child.*

Chapter 3

Introductions

Theron opened his eyes as he heard a ringing sound to his left. He rolled over on the bed to see what was making the noise and realized it was the phone on the nightstand. He reached over and lifted the phone off its stand, putting the receiver to his ear.

"Hello," Theron said into the phone.

"Oh good, you're awake Mr. Zeyla. This is Ms. Norris at the front desk. I figured you might have been too tired yesterday to set an alarm, so I'm giving you a wakeup call. You have an hour and a half to get ready for the opening ceremony. Also, a couple members from the Tailoring Club came by after you retired to your room yesterday and delivered your uniforms. You can come up to the front desk to get them."

It took Theron a few moments to register what the dorm mother was saying, but when he looked at the clock and saw the time he jumped out of bed. "Oh, sorry! I didn't realize I'd slept so long. Thank you for being so thoughtful."

Theron heard a chuckle come over the phone. "It's okay. I'll be waiting here with your uniforms."

"All right, I'll head right over to pick them up," Theron responded before hanging up the phone. He was still dressed from when he had laid down to take a nap. His clothes looked wrinkled, but he didn't have anything else to change into yet. He felt a little embarrassed, but there was no other choice but to head to the front desk in what he was wearing. He made sure he had his keycards before leaving the room.

When he arrived at the front desk Ms. Norris gave him a grin. It was obvious she could tell at a glance he had slept in his clothes, but she was kind enough not to mention it as she beckoned him to come behind the desk. "Here are your uniforms. The Tailoring Club also brought two pairs of shoes, they're in these bags."

"Thank you," Theron said as he grabbed hold of all the hangers for the clothes in one hand and picked up the bags with the shoes in his other hand. "Well, I'm going to go get ready. Thanks again for the wakeup call."

Ms. Norris smiled and waved at Theron as he walked back to his room. He hung up his uniforms in his closet and thought about which one to wear. Based on how cool the spring mountain air had felt, he decided to wear one of the blazer uniforms instead of one with a sweater vest. He also remembered that he was going to be introduced to the student body at the opening ceremony. Theron really didn't want to stand out any more than he had to, so he decided to wear the more traditional navy blue blazer, even though his personal preference would have been to wear the crimson color. He did decide to wear a red tie though. After selecting his clothes, he put them towards the bathroom side of the closet and proceeded to take a shower. He was ready within thirty minutes.

With about forty-five minutes remaining until the opening ceremony, Theron left the dorm and headed towards the dining hall. He noticed other students heading in the same direction. Most of them were wearing the same style of outfit he was, but the colors of the blazers seemed to be completely based on personal preference. Only a few others were wearing the navy blue he had chosen. Most were in colors not included in the uniforms he'd been given. He started regretting not choosing the crimson blazer, but decided to take it as a lesson that he should go with his own preferences rather than ignoring them for the sake of blending in.

When Theron arrived at the dining hall he began looking for either Katerina or Deacon, but there were too many students walking around for him to pick out either one from the crowd. Rather than waste all his time looking, he proceeded to select his breakfast from the buffet. After he turned away from the buffet, he saw Katerina walking up to him. She must have spotted him while he was getting his food.

"Good morning Theron. I see you got your uniform. How did everything else go yesterday?" Katerina asked.

Theron thought about what he should and shouldn't let her know about before he responded. "It was pretty fast paced at first. Apparently Doctor Vaashti is going to have me visit her every day to observe me. I also got checked into my room finally, but I fell asleep shortly after that. I only meant to take a short nap, but instead I just woke up not too long ago. Oh, I also have the number to call me directly. I wanted to give you a copy." Theron fished around in his pocket for a slip of paper he had written his number on while he was getting ready.

Katerina took the paper with a happy smile. "Oh thanks, I'll call you later and give you my number." Then her voice took on a concerned tone. "So did the doctor find anything that made her want to keep you under observation?"

"No, actually it's the opposite. She said people don't

just fall into comas and then just wake up for no reason, so she wants to observe me so she can try to identify the original cause. I'm really not happy about it." Theron sighed. "Anyway, have you seen the Student Council President? I wanted to find out what I'm supposed to do during the opening ceremony."

"The Student Council is in the auditorium. I guess we'd better hurry up and eat so you can go over there." Before, Katerina would have pouted at the suggestion that he had to leave her alone, but it seems their conversation yesterday had put some of her worries at ease. She wasn't acting as clingy, which was a bit of a relief to Theron, but also a little disappointing.

Katerina had already finished half her meal before she had come over to Theron, but they finished about the same time since he was in a bit of a rush. "All right, I'm going to head over to the auditorium now. I don't know if I'll be able to see you during the ceremony, but we can meet after if you'd like."

Katerina nodded. "Okay, let's meet up in front of the high school. The classroom assignments will be posted outside, so we can meet there."

"I'll see you there then," Theron said before taking off towards the auditorium.

He arrived about twenty minutes before the opening ceremony was supposed to begin. There were already numerous students of all ages finding their seats. Theron walked towards the stage. As he approached, he noticed a couple of students, a boy and a girl, wearing uniforms in the same shade of royal blue that Deacon's blazer had been when Theron first met him. He figured they were also members of the Student Council, so he decided to call out to them. "Excuse me, I'm Theron Zeyla, the special scholarship student for this year. Do you know what I'm supposed to be doing? President Cynan told me I was supposed to be introduced to everyone today, but I'm not sure where I should be for that."

The girl turned towards him first. "Oh, so you're Theron. We've been told to expect you. I'm the Student Council Secretary, Elizabeth Aceldama. And this is the Student Council Treasurer, Raul Gaspare."

Raul held out his hand. "Nice to meet you, Theron."

Theron shook Raul's hand then turned back towards Elizabeth. "It's a pleasure to meet you both. Deacon, I mean President Cynan, told me he wanted to introduce me to the members of the Student Council. How many others are there?"

"Just the vice-president. She's with the president backstage." Elizabeth gestured for Theron to go meet them.

"Thank you. I'm sure I'll see you later," Theron said as he proceeded backstage.

There were a lot of adults around backstage. Theron assumed they were members of the faculty. It didn't take him long to find Deacon among the adults. "Hello Deacon. The secretary, Elizabeth, sent me back here. I hope I'm not bothering you while you're busy."

Deacon turned toward Theron. "Oh no, it's fine. I already have my speech memorized. So you've already met Liz and Raul, I guess that just leaves Ady." Deacon turned towards another girl in the royal blue Student Council uniform and called out, "Ady! Come over here. There's someone I want you to meet."

The girl shot a glare towards Deacon and walked over to him. "I keep telling you not to call me that, especially not in public."

Deacon shrugged. "But your name is too much trouble to say. Besides, Ady means noble, so it's still fitting, right? Anyway, this is Theron Zeyla, the special scholarship student."

The girl looked at Theron carefully before offering her hand. "It's a pleasure to meet you, Theron. My name is Adrasteia Narkissa. I know it can be a mouth full, but I'd appreciate it if you didn't give me any nicknames."

Theron took her hand. "Don't worry. I'm not as laid back as President Cynan, so I wouldn't call you something that upsets you. Besides, I'm not really one for nicknames."

Deacon grinned at the exchange between the two. "Well, now that the formalities are out of the way, we might as well just hang out here and wait for our turns. Oh, and don't worry Theron, we won't make you give an impromptu speech or anything like that. I'll be the one to introduce you, so when I call your name just come out and take a bow, and I'll do all the talking."

Theron nodded. "Okay."

It wasn't a very long wait before everything seemed to quiet down, and a man with graying hair walked up the podium. "Welcome everyone to New Babel Academy. For those of you that do not know me, I'm Mr. Zupan, the principal and head of the faculty at this academy. Though my office is located in the high school building, my door is always open for our elementary and junior high students as well.

"Many of you already know each other, and have made friends. I hope you all continue to strengthen those friendships in the year to come, but also remember not to forsake the opportunity to make new friendships as well. The academics you will learn here can be learned in many other schools, or can be taught by tutors at your homes, but the chances you have to form relationships here are a once-in-a-lifetime opportunity. Those relationships are the reason you are here. You are all members of the elite of society. You have every opportunity afforded to you. It is my hope that, while you are here, you will learn to make the most of those opportunities for the sake of the future.

"New Babel Academy was named based on that ideal. The original Tower of Babel was built in ancient times to be a beacon that would hold humanity together. So too do we wish for New Babel Academy to be the first step in bringing the world together as one. The other faculty members and I put great hopes and expectations upon you all. You are the future of this world."

"God, this is already getting boring," Deacon whispered from behind Theron's shoulder. "Why do people giving a speech feel they have to go on and on about things when a few words will do the same job?"

"Well, I imagine it helps the students get a feel for what he's like. After all, I don't think many of them would have regular contact with the principal," Theron suggested.

Deacon scoffed, "More like it makes him feel important. He's really just a figurehead. The Student Council and the chairwoman have all the real power in the school. Still, you may have a point regarding the new kids that don't know how things work around here. They're used to adults having all the authority, so maybe it's somewhat comforting to uphold that illusion at first. At least, it would be if they had the attention spans needed to sit through all of it."

Theron couldn't really argue. "I'm reminded of a story I heard about Abraham Lincoln and the Gettysburg Address. It was about how the speaker before Lincoln, Edward Everett I believe, delivered a two hour oratory that was meant to be the Gettysburg Address that day. Shortly after, Lincoln gave his speech that lasted only a few minutes. It so overshadowed the former speaker that Everett felt compelled to write Lincoln a letter after the address. In the letter, Everett basically said he wished he could flatter himself by believing he came as near to the central idea of the occasion, in two hours, as Lincoln did in two minutes."

"See, speeches should be left short and sweet." Deacon nodded. "Or at least, if it can't be short, it should be to the point."

"Would you two be quiet," Adrasteia hissed.

The three stood together in silence as the principal continued his speech. Eventually, he got around to introducing the faculty members and making general announcements before finally wrapping up his speech. "Now, I present to you all your Student Council President, Deacon Cynan."

Deacon clapped Theron on the shoulder before heading out on stage. Applause was sporadic as Deacon stepped up to the podium. "WAKE UP EVERYBODY!" He yelled with enthusiasm. He had kept his distance from the microphone to make sure that the speaker system didn't squeal with the sudden noise. Theron could hear a renewed clamoring from the audience.

"That's better." Deacon nodded. "Good morning everyone. As many of you know, I'm the Student Council President, Deacon Cynan. I'd like to start off by introducing you to the other members of the Student Council." The students Theron had just recently introduced himself to walked out on stage as their names were called. "First, the Student Council Vice-President, Adrasteia Narkissa. Next, your Student Council Secretary, Elizabeth Aceldama. And finally, your Student Council Treasurer, Raul Gaspare." There was a roar of applause as all the members of the Student Council bowed. The atmosphere seemed to be changing to more of a rock concert. Theron could only be in awe of how popular this Student Council must be on campus.

"We members of the Student Council are your representatives," Deacon continued after the audience had quieted down some. "If you have any complaints or suggestions about things on campus, please let us know. We have suggestion boxes located at every facility on campus. Also, if you want to praise something or someone on campus, let us hear that too. We use the public opinion of the organizations on campus when setting up budgets and giving perks like preferential placements during campus fairs. Even though we've been chosen by you all as the leaders of this academy, we want to make sure you never forget that we are also one of you. We are all students of New Babel Academy, and on that topic, I have someone else to introduce. A special new student is going to be joining us this year. He is the special scholarship student that we, your Student Council, have selected, and he has the full backing of our chairwoman, the founder of this academy. I'd like to present to you all a new second year high school student: Theron Zeyla."

Theron took his cue to walk out on stage and stand next to the other members of the Student Council. There was a wave of applause, not as energetic as the one for the Student Council President, but this time it was accompanied by a wave of murmuring voices as people discussed the presence of a special scholarship student. Theron made his bow to the student body. He had probably never been more nervous than he was at that moment.

Deacon continued his introductions after he saw Theron finish his bow. "Theron is the first student in history to max out the applicant exam, but he's not just smart." Deacon paused to make sure the students attention was back on him. "I have to be honest with you all. I abused my position as the Student Council

President to get to know Theron ahead of you all." Deacon hung his head in mock shame, turning his introduction into a performance. Next he shot his head up and reached out his hand towards the audience. "But I did it for you all! So I could report my findings to you!"

Deacon took the microphone off its stand and walked over to Theron. "This boy isn't just smart. After spending time with him, I can tell you he's also kind and courteous. Every now and then you'll see a bit of a mischievous glint in his eyes, even though he seems so serious most of the time. He's also very driven and dedicated. In short, I can promise you that getting to know him will be a rewarding experience."

Deacon reached out and shook Theron's hand in front of everyone before returning to the podium. "Well, I could go on and on with announcements and such, but I don't want to waste all of your time, so I'll just remind you all to check the bulletin boards in front of each of your schools. It's the primary method we, as the Student Council, will use to communicate with you all, so please make sure to check it regularly. Now, without further ado, it's time I introduce to you all the founder of our school. Madam Chairwoman, the floor is yours." Deacon turned toward the backstage area and bowed.

The chairwoman walked out on stage gently patting Deacon on the shoulder as she stepped up to the podium. "Thank you for the entertaining introductions, President Cynan. Members of the Student Council, I look forward to working with you again in the coming months. I know you are already hard at work, so I won't hold you here." The Student Council members bowed to the chairwoman before they left the stage. Theron took the chance to follow along with them. Once he was backstage again, Theron turned to listen to the chairwoman's speech.

The chairwoman addressed the students. "I don't plan on keeping you much longer. I just had one topic I wanted to talk to you all about. During your time at this academy, I want you all to carefully consider the school crest. Each part is symbolic of what it means to be a student of this academy, of what it means to be a true member of the elite. The rose, wrapped around the hilt of the sword that drips with blood, is a symbol of beauty. The sword itself, a symbol of the power each of you will wield when you go out into this world as adults. The blood that symbolizes both the bloodlines you are a part of, and the lives you will be responsible for."

The chairwoman began a more detailed explanation of how the symbols were related. "The rose wraps around the sword to symbolize the idea that beauty and compassion should always sheathe your power. As elites, you must all learn to act with grace and charisma to achieve your goals before you resort to using the power of your station. It is a simple matter to resort to forceful methods. That alone doesn't make you special. Learn to interact with the soft sweetness of a rose. Also note how the thorns of the vine wrap around the hilt. Your power is not to be grasped by others. It is for you alone, do not allow others to use you.

"As I already mentioned, the sword is a symbol of power. Just as resorting to force alone is not the way of a true elite, one cannot call themselves elite without power. The sword is essential to your identity, but it is not a tactless instrument. A sword must be used with precision, for both offense and defense. So too should you learn to use your resources. Mastery is an ongoing process, and you should never stop learning the best ways to apply the powers you have been given.

"Finally, the blood. Remember that in the end, your power affects real people. It is the lives of countless individuals that dance at your whim. The blood is also a symbol of your lineage. None of you are the founders of your fortunes. Some of you come from long established families with ancient traditions, others of you are the first step in establishing your own family dynasties. All of you together will form a new age of aristocracy, where it is not your relation to a sovereign, but your ability to manage resources, or affect the hearts of the masses, that makes you an elite. Keep those things in your heart, and wear your academy's crest with pride as a reminder of not only how special you are, but how amazing you can be. I hope you can walk the path to become true elites together, working with one another to create a better future, and with that hope I send you forth to your new school year. The opening ceremony is now over. Students, please report to your schools to find out your class assignments, then report to your homerooms."

With that statement, the chairwoman left the stage. The speech left Theron feeling a little left out. After all, he had spent the last six years in an orphanage. He didn't have any power. His parents were dead, so he had no idea how to uphold any bloodline he may have. Theron shook the negative thoughts from his head. He couldn't linger on the past. Everything would begin from here.

The faculty had already left the backstage area, probably heading towards their classes to wait for their students. Theron left to meet up with Katerina outside the high school. Like before, there were other students on the path, but this time they started calling out to him. Theron tried to be courteous, offering polite waves and smiles, or making agreeable comments when someone might call out hoping they were in the same class. By the time he had reached the high school he was already starting to feel a little hounded, but another part of him felt satisfied by all the attention.

As Theron neared the crowd of students around a board set up outside the school, Katerina ran up to him smiling. "We're in the same class!" She cried out happily.

"That's a relief." Theron smiled back at her. "Shall we go to class together?"

"Yes!" Katerina responded and grabbed Theron's hand as they walked together. Theron could hear murmurs around him as people looked at the two of them. Some of those murmurs sounded a little jealous, but Katerina didn't seem to pay any attention to them.

They reached the classroom marked 2-B and entered. "Come on in and take whichever seat you like," the teacher said while standing at the podium. On the board behind him the name 'Mr. Lehrer' had been written. No other students were in the classroom yet.

"Where would you like to sit?" Theron asked Katerina.

"Umm, I think somewhere in a corner," Katerina answered.

"In that case, how about you take that back seat next to the window, and I'll sit next to you?" Theron suggested.

"That sounds good to me." Katerina nodded. The two sat next to each other. Theron stretched out on his desk and put his head down, waiting for other students to come in.

He didn't have to wait long before several students came in. The way they were talking indicated they all knew each other. One of them seemed to notice Theron and Katerina. "Oh, there he is! Katerina! Why are you sitting next to him? You don't even like hanging out with people."

Katerina gripped her hands till they turned white before she responded. "Hello Alessia. He's my friend, so naturally I wanted to sit next to him."

"You have a friend? And it just happens to be the special scholarship student? Don't you dare go trying to get ahead of us Katerina! It'll be major points if we can be friends with him. Maybe even enough to get us into A class." Alessia seemed to be building up to hysterics.

"You know, I did have a say in it too," Theron said dryly, reminding the others that he was present.

Alessia seemed mortified by the comment. She must have realized that she had just declared that becoming his friend would be purely for a selfish benefit, but she didn't mention it as she tried to explain herself. "I'm so sorry, I didn't mean any offense, it's just that we used to try to be friends with Katerina in the past, but she always seemed to reject us. I'm just so shocked that she'd claim to be friends with you."

"Don't worry about it. I'm not really sure what it is she likes about me, but I'm glad that she chose to be my friend. That being said, it's not like I'm not allowed to have other friends too, right?" Theron looked towards Katerina.

"Of course, but I still want to be your closest friend," Katerina said it with a determined look that was only slightly spoiled by her blushing.

"I don't mind that." Theron turned back towards Alessia and all the other students that had come over with her. "I guess you all already know who I am thanks to that spectacle the president put on, but I'm looking forward to getting to know each of you this year."

"I'm glad you all are starting to get along, but I'm afraid it's about time to get the orientation started," Mr. Lehrer cut in. "Everyone please take a seat." All the other students quietly picked out seats, sat down, and waited for the teacher to continue. "Okay, first, is there anyone who either volunteers or wants to nominate someone to be the class representative?"

"I want to volunteer." Alessia raised her hand.

"All right, anyone else?" Mr. Lehrer asked. One of the boys raised his hand. "Oh, perfect. We have a male and female. I'll let you two decide which of you will take what responsibilities."

The boy responded, "I don't mind being the sub representative. You can be in charge of all the meetings and scheduling, Alessia."

"Okay, thanks Darian," Alessia agreed.

"So, Miss Alessia Caito will be the main representative. You can lead the class from here in selecting the class duties," Mr. Lehrer concluded and sat down in a chair in the corner facing the students.

"Okay." Alessia got up and walked to the blackboard. "If it's all right with everyone, we'll have the day duty rotate on a schedule. There are ten of us in class, so we'll have two on duty each day." No one voiced any objections. "Okay, next we have the other class officers. Does anyone want to be the committee representative for school activities? Or should we decide on a different one for each event?"

"I will do it Alessia. At least for the first event." Another boy raised his hand.

"Okay, Nicholas will be the first committee representative. We'll select the next representative after the first event." Alessia wrote his name on the board along with his role. "Next up is the class tactician."

"Class tactician?" Theron couldn't help calling out. What could a school class need a tactician for?

"Oh, I guess this school is unique in that regard. The classes here compete with one another in a bunch of different events, so usually each class appoints a tactician to be in charge of gathering intelligence on the other classes and developing strategies," Alessia explained.

"I'll do it, of course," another boy said, "but I'd like Kaitlyn to be my assistant."

"All right, Vincent is going to be the tactician. Kaitlyn, would you mind assisting him?"

"No, I don't mind," one of the girls answered.

Alessia wrote down the names on the board. "Okay, next is the health officer."

"About that," Mr. Lehrer interrupted, "I got a request from Doctor Vaashti for Mr. Zeyla to be the health officer."

"What? She requested him specifically? This is an outrage!" Another boy, who had been silent until now, exclaimed as he stood up.

Mr. Lehrer shrugged. "I was told she couldn't divulge her reasons due to doctor patient confidentiality. I suppose you can make of that what you will."

"What, the new kid has a disease or something so he gets to be the health officer?" the boy complained.

"There's nothing you can do about it, Jacques. It was a request from the doctor herself," Alessia stated, cutting Jacques off. "Theron will be the male health officer, but we'll need a female officer too for certain delicate situations." Katerina and another girl both raised their hands. "Katerina and Hikari both want the position. Does either of you want to back down?"

The girl, Hikari, smiled towards Katerina. "Oh, I'm surprised you're even willing to start participating in the class this much. I'd be more than happy to step aside for you."

"Thank you Hikari, I know you've always been one of the health officers, and I'm sorry for being so selfish in suddenly trying to take over." Katerina bowed her head.

"Oh don't worry about it Katerina, I'm happy enough to see you take a more active role," Hikari answered.

"So that's settled then?" Alessia waited for confirmation nods before adding Theron's and Katerina's names to the board. "Finally we have the class prefect."

"That's a role I was born for." A large boy stood up with a smile.

"You don't need to get so excited, Alonzo," Alessia stated flatly and stared at Alonzo until he sat down. "I assume there are no other volunteers? In that case Alonzo will be the prefect, and that's all the official roles. Of course everyone should feel free to assist each other as the situation allows. Please consider the appointed officers just the leaders in their assigned roles. We should all work together to make this class the best in the school. Mr. Lehrer, do you have anything else for us?"

Mr. Lehrer got up from his seat. "It's nice being in charge of a class that's been together for a while. You all assigned your roles pretty quickly. As you all know, classes start tomorrow at eight o'clock in the morning. In each of your desks you'll find your course syllabi so you can read any material you need to before class tomorrow. Club meetings are starting at two o'clock this afternoon. For those of you not in clubs, you are free for the rest of the day. Mr. Zeyla and Miss Aikia, as the health officers you'll need to meet with Doctor Vaashti today. That's all I have for you right now, so class is dismissed."

"All rise," Alessia instructed. Everyone stood up. "Bow." All the students bowed to Mr. Lehrer, who then exited the room. It was a show of respect that Theron hadn't seen before, but he didn't mind it as a way of disciplining one's mind to receive instruction.

"So, I guess we should head over to the doctor's office," Katerina said to Theron.

"Sure," Theron agreed.

"Wait you two, why don't we all go together to the dining hall for lunch? It's on your way anyway," Alessia said, looking around to get everyone's agreement. No one opposed her as they got up and collected their things.

"I don't have a problem with that," Theron said. Katerina simply nodded.

Everyone walked to the dining hall together, most of them chatting about how things went during their break from school. A few asked Theron some questions about his thoughts on various things, but no one tried to pry into his past, for which he was grateful. Some of them even asked Katerina some questions, as if testing to see how much her new found interest in other people would go. She answered all the questions courteously, but Theron could tell she was feeling awkward and tense.

Once they arrived at the dining hall they temporarily split up. Some of them had ordered meals, but most went to the buffet like Katerina and Theron did.

"You know, the buffet was originally used by French nobility as a way to display their wealth," Jacques commented.

"Oh, that would explain why it isn't spelled how it sounds," Theron quipped. He could hear a few of his classmates snicker at the comment.

"Well, it is only natural that the French should have a more elegant way of pronouncing words than the rest of the world," Jacques responded.

"If that's the case, they must also have a different set of ears to match," Nicholas teased.

"Nicholas, Jacques, Theron. Stop picking on each other and finish getting your food. It won't be long before other students start coming," Alessia commanded. The three boys all did as they were told.

Everyone gathered at a round table big enough for all of them to sit at.

"Well, I'm glad that Theron isn't too formal to make a joke. To be honest, I was a little intimidated to learn that the special scholarship student would be in our class," the girl named Kaitlyn commented.

"True enough, it's good to see you starting to fit in." Darian, the new sub class representative, nodded encouragingly towards Theron.

"Well, I for one am fired up to have a new challenger in our class rankings," Alonzo said with a grin.

Vincent clapped Theron on the back. "I couldn't agree more, and I won't let myself be beaten, even if you are the special scholarship student."

"Well, I really don't think I'm all that special, but I'll try to do my best to work with everyone, especially in those class competitions you all mentioned. Those sound like fun," Theron answered everyone's comments.

The banter continued in much the same manner as they ate together, but eventually the dining hall was starting to get too loud with all the students starting to come in for lunch. Most of them seemed to be talking about their hopes for the new year, or getting to know new classmates.

When Theron finished eating he excused himself and told Katerina he'd be waiting outside for her. He didn't have to wait very long before she came out to meet him. "Sorry to keep you waiting," Katerina apologized.

"It's no problem, and I'm sorry to leave you back there. I just don't like being in places with a lot of noise. It makes it feel like my skull is being squeezed by too much pressure," Theron explained. "Anyway, shall we go see the doctor?"

"Lead the way." Katerina followed Theron as he walked through the sliding glass door into the medical facility. Together they walked to Doctor Vaashti's door and knocked.

"Come in," a voice instructed from inside.

Theron opened the door and entered with Katerina still following. "We were told to report to you as the health officers from Class 2-B," Theron stated. There was still some tension in his voice, and in trying to cover it up he ended up sounding a bit monotone.

"I was expecting Mr. Zeyla, but I'm sorry, what was your name again?" Doctor Vaashti asked Katerina.

"My name is Katerina Aikia," Katerina responded.

The doctor nodded. "All right. Mr. Zeyla, Miss Aikia, there really isn't a whole lot I need to tell you both. Your primary duty is to escort people who need to use our facilities, and to monitor those people while you are escorting them so you can report symptoms, or lack thereof, to whatever medical professional is present."

Doctor Vaashti opened a drawer in her desk and pulled out two keys. "I'll give you both keys to the cabinets containing basic first aid equipment so you can put disinfectants and band aids on people with minor injuries. Never, under any circumstance, administer any drugs without the instruction of a professional. That's really all you have to keep in mind for your duties. Every Saturday, I'll have all the health officers gather for brief meetings. I'll leave it to you all to decide if you want to do any extra activities, like health awareness fairs and things like that."

"Okay, if that's everything, are we free to go now?" Theron asked.

"Miss Aikia can go, but I need to ask you a few questions," Doctor Vaashti responded to Theron.

"I'll wait outside if it's something private," Katerina

offered.

"Oh, I don't really have anything to hide from her. I don't mind if she stays if it's just answering a few questions." Theron really wasn't comfortable with the idea of being alone with the doctor.

"You two really are close." Doctor Vaashti frowned briefly before going on. "What hospital did you go to when you were at your home?"

"I didn't go to a hospital while I was living in the orphanage," Theron answered. "I don't think I've been to a hospital in over twelve years. My parents always had doctors come to them while they were ill, and I don't know which hospital they came from."

Doctor Vaashti nodded, not really surprised by the answer. "Then let's go with another approach. Do you know what hospital you were born in?"

"I don't remember which hospital, but I was born in Berlin. My parents had spent a lot of time there when they were still working, so they decided to stay there after they retired," Theron answered.

"Do you know if there were any complications with your birth?" the doctor asked.

Theron thought for a moment. "From what my parents told me, I was born with an extremely weak body. Apparently the doctors didn't think I'd live very long. But within a few months I had stabilized and by the time I was four I was considered in excellent health."

"I see." Doctor Vaashti looked like she was lost in her thoughts for a moment. "I think that's enough information for me to find your medical records. That's all I needed to ask you for now. You can both go."

Theron nodded and headed out the door. Once he was in the hallway, Katerina tugged on his blazer. Theron turned to her and saw her looking at him with sad eyes. "I didn't know that your parents had died, or that you'd been raised in an orphanage. I guess that's what you meant when you said your parents' position wouldn't mean anything."

"Yes," Theron answered, "but they've been dead for over six years now. I still miss them, but it's not like I'm torn up about it. They knew they were going to die in advance, so they had some time to prepare me for that. As for being raised in an orphanage, I'm sorry if I betrayed your expectations. I'm not really an elite anymore, just another orphan wandering through the world."

Katerina shook her head. "That's not true. It doesn't really matter where you were raised. What matters is what you make of yourself, and I told you before, remember, that you are someone with the talents to reach the top of the professional world on your own. You're a true elite, not someone that's following in the footsteps of others, but someone who has the power to forge their own path. If anything, I think you're even more wonderful to have made it this far after suffering so much."

Theron smiled at her. "Thanks Katerina. Anyway, I need to get back to my room and start studying for tomorrow, and you need to get back so you can call me and give me your number."

"Oh that's right!" Katerina exclaimed. Apparently she'd forgotten that Theron had given her his number already. "Well then, I'll call you in about thirty minutes. How about while we're studying we each write down the points we think are important and then we can share them over dinner. You did say you'd help me study after all."

Theron nodded. "All right, let's do that. I'll be anticipating your call then." They split up as they left the cultural center, each heading towards their own dormitory. Theron was still worried about everything he was being dragged into regarding the psychic vampire, but for some reason, it didn't seem as troubling as it was yesterday. Having Katerina with him was a great support. Theron also found it odd that the more time he spent with the doctor, Trish Vaashti, the more he got the feeling she wasn't that bad of a person. It made no sense, but he had learned to trust his instincts over the years when he had to fend for himself, so he couldn't simply dismiss the feeling. Perhaps the next few weeks would bring him the answers he needed.

Chapter 4

Preparations

Class 2-B had all gathered together in the dining hall for lunch. It had only been a couple weeks since the term had started, but this was already part of the class's routine. What wasn't routine was the topic of conversation. Earlier that day the first competitive event had been announced. It was scheduled to be held in three weeks.

Vincent, the class tactician, started briefing the class. "Okay everyone, Nicholas, as a member of the event committee, has informed us that the first event is going to be primarily an athletic competition, though there will be other disciplines added to certain events to help level the playing field. Also, even though all classes will be competing against each other in each event, the scores will be awarded by academic year, so if a third year beats you it's no big deal. Just don't let another second year beat you. Nicholas, would you be able to explain the individual competitions for us?"

Nicholas nodded. "There are going to be five categories of competitions. We're calling the first category 'artistic athleticism'. There will be three competitions: figure skating, gymnastics, and dancing. Each class will compete in two of the three events with different participants in each event, and the scores will be normalized for comparisons. Also, all three events will require both a male and female participant. The class with the highest combined rating will win the category. Each place within the category will be worth an inverse number of points to the placement. So if there are four places awarded in a grade level, first place gets four points, second place gets three points, and so on.

"The second category is a track meet. I won't go into all the individual events, but there are no field events to worry about, just the running events. Basically we should generally just assign people by the type of running they're best at. Unlike the artistic category, if we wanted to we could have the same person do all the events, or we could try to spread out the events amongst everyone. We could also forfeit any events we choose. Each placement within the top three of an event is worth a set number of points, so first place would be worth five points, second place three points, and third place would be worth just one point. The class with the most points at the end wins the category, and each class will be awarded category points along the same lines as before.

"The third category is the endurance competition. This is where the different strategies of the classes will really start to show. There won't be a very long break between the track meet and the endurance events, so if we pursue the track meet too aggressively, we may be too tired to have a shot at winning this category. There are three events, and they are brutal. There is a one hour decathlon, in which the participant must start the last of the ten events, the 1,500-meter run, within one hour of starting the first event, the 100-meter dash. There is also going to be a marathon. The third event will be an Olympic distance triathlon. Each class must participate in all three events, and the races will be held concurrently. The times for the triathlon and marathon will be converted into points in the same way the events of the decathlon are, with lower times being awarded more points. The class with the most combined points wins the category.

"The fourth category is a swimming competition. Its format is going to be very similar to the track meet, with a lot of events and no restrictions on how we assign participants. I don't expect any problems there, but the fifth category is a different matter. It's a single event: an obstacle race. Only one participant from each class is allowed. Before a participant can go through a stage of the course they must answer a series of academic questions. There will be no indication of whether the answer is right or wrong during the event. Each incorrect answer will cause ten seconds to be added to your final time.

"The winner of the fifth category will not receive the normal points for winning the category. Instead, they will earn double any category points earned in the entire competition. Basically, if a class wins the fifth category and gets second or third in all the other categories they'll win the overall competition. All other places in the final category get no points, so it's set up as a winner-take-all reward. Also, I should add that in all categories where an imbalance may exist between male and female participants, their scores will also be normalized. We haven't worked out exactly how much to adjust each event, but I can assure you it will be fair using a lot of statistical data from races in each age group. That's all the information I'm allowed to give for now. Keep in mind I won't be able to participate since I'm part of the committee," Nicholas concluded his explanation.

Everyone just looked at each other before Vincent

took charge of the meeting again. "Well, as you can guess from hearing all that, this is going to be a brutal competition. Given that all the classes are pretty small, it's really going to put pressure on everyone, especially towards the end. Since genders will be normalized, we should just assign everyone according to what they're best at. Most of you I already have an idea about, but I don't know how good Theron is athletically."

"I'm not a good swimmer, or rather I'm not very experienced. The same goes for any of the first category events," Theron admitted, "but I'm confident I can do well in everything else Nicholas mentioned."

Vincent nodded. "Okay, I'll have to test you later to be sure, but I don't want anyone else to see. I'm not going to announce who will be doing what, but I'll let each of you know your roles privately. The week before the competition we're having an extended weekend where we'll be allowed to go home for five days. I recommend most of you do your intensive training then. The less people know about our overall plan and the physical conditions of our team members the better. That being said, I think everyone will be able to guess that Theron will be participating in the obstacle race, given his academic abilities. Even if he doesn't do great on the obstacles themselves, he'll probably be able to make up the difference with that monster brain of his."

"That's true," Darian commented. "I've been meaning to ask you, Theron. How do you know so much? Your results from that preliminary test we had last week were insane. Who gets perfect scores on material that hasn't been covered yet?"

"Oh, well it wasn't exactly new material to me," Theron explained. "Due to my circumstances growing up, I had a lot of free time, so I ended up reading everything I could get my hands on. Along the way I also found out I have an abnormally good memory, so I'll remember anything I see or hear. I eventually got to the point where I'd listen to an audiobook while reading a different book, so I ended up learning a lot of things pretty quickly. Though what amazes me is that this academy teaches up to a college level in math and science by third year in junior high, just so you can focus on economics and political science in high school."

"Well, I guess in that regard we're not so different, though we didn't learn on our own," Alessia commented. "Most of us have tutors to supplement our core curriculum. The academy expects that, so it allows them to rush through the material in most classes. Still, learning Keynesian economics this year after learning classical economics last year is giving me a headache."

"I hear third years have it even worse. They're asked to find the flaws in the modern forms of both systems and try to come up with improvements or even complete revisions. I understand the need for a basic grasp on economics, but I'm going to be taking over my family's business some day. I don't need to be a full-fledged economist when I can just hire one if I need to," Alonzo complained.

"Well, it doesn't hurt to know those things yourself either," Hikari responded to the complaint. "Even if you hire someone to keep track of trends and suggest ideas for your company's fiscal policy, you still need to understand where that person is coming from so you will know whether or not you can trust the advice given."

"Well, we'll learn whatever we're asked to learn anyway, so there's no point going on about it," Alessia said. "Though getting back to Theron, I'm curious why you come to class every day. Even the teachers have told you that you were excused from classes for the next few weeks since you already knew the material."

Theron shrugged. "To be honest, I wouldn't know what to do with myself anyway. Besides, since I promised to help Katerina study, I figured I should attend class so I can know in more detail what the lectures are covering. If I just go from the syllabi and my own understanding of the topics I might miss something that could be important for her."

"You're teaching Katerina? That's so not fair," Kaitlyn protested. "You should hold study sessions for all of us."

"Speak for yourself. I for one have no interest in learning from him." Jacques turned up his nose at the thought. He had been hostile toward Theron since their first day of classes, and didn't show any interest in improving their relationship, but Theron didn't really care. He had been hated by people before, and he wasn't the type that tried to make people friends, but for some reason, most people did like him.

"Hey Jacques, that's going too far. He's obviously the best student in the class. It'll improve the class average and make us all look better. Why do you have to be such a pain?" Alessia was practically growling at Jacques.

"He can't help it, Alessia. It's hardwired into his DNA," Nicholas said dryly.

"Count on the Englishman to not understand self-pride," Jacques shot back at Nicholas.

"Okay you two, that's enough. No international feuds on campus, remember?" Darian lightly chastised the two.

"Well, getting back to Kaitlyn's comment, I don't really mind helping out with studies every now and then for those that want it," Theron said as he got up from the table. "Personally, I'd prefer to help you individually rather than a group study session. I don't enjoy feeling like a lecturer. Anyway, I'm going to report to Doctor Vaashti."

Katerina got up from the table as well. "I'll come too."

Everyone but Jacques gave courteous parting words. Jacques just half glared at Theron. Thanks to the class formats for the high school students, required classes were held during the morning, but after lunch everyone was free to take elective classes which often either tied into club activities or supplemented the core curriculum. Enrolling in electives was technically optional, but strongly encouraged. Theron hadn't figured out what he wanted to do yet for his electives, so his afternoons were mostly free. Katerina seemed to be in the same situation, so she usually just hung out with him.

Lately he had been spending more time with Doctor Vaashti. He had almost begun to doubt what he'd seen on his first night here, though he hadn't voiced that thought to Uma yet. Still, he knew that the doctor wasn't human. Even from the first moment Theron had seen her, something about the doctor had felt supernatural, but now that he had spent a few weeks training his psychic abilities with Uma, he couldn't ignore the inhuman aura around Trish Vaashti. The question that came to his mind most often now was whether simply being inhuman was enough to make someone evil. Doctor Vaashti had made no hostile actions that he could see, and no more attacks had occurred on campus since the one he'd witnessed. Then there were his instincts that continued to tell him that something was off about that night, that maybe the doctor had her reasons for doing what she did. He really didn't know what to make of the doctor, so he ended up spending more time with her, trying to figure her out.

Of course, Katerina always went with him.

However, as Theron had started spending more time with his visits, it seemed that the doctor was becoming annoyed by Katerina. It wasn't extreme enough to be called rude, but the doctor would make little comments every now and then that suggested she was getting tired of Katerina always tagging along when she didn't really need to be there. In response, Katerina had become a little standoffish with Doctor Vaashti as well.

"Umm, before we go the doctor, I want to ask you something," Katerina said hesitantly, bringing Theron out of his thoughts.

"What is it?" Theron asked.

Katerina fidgeted a bit before asking, "In the break we have coming up, if you don't have anywhere else to go, would you like to come visit my parents' house? I can't imagine you'll be able to train very well if you go back to your home, and it might be lonely here all by yourself."

Theron frowned. "That place isn't really a home. Besides, if I went back there it's possible I wouldn't be able to return." He paused before going on. He decided to tease her a little bit. "I don't know if I really need to train anyway, and besides, I'm used to being alone." Theron waited to see her expression wilt before he said, "Then again, I did promise myself after hearing you'd been left alone before that I wouldn't leave you like that. So if you'll be lonely without me then I guess I have no choice. I'll go with you."

Katerina's eyes widened for a few moments before she scowled, though Theron could tell she was trying to hide a smile. "You can be so mean sometimes. Do you like to see me depressed that much?"

Theron averted his gaze as he answered, "Well, I admit I do get a little happy seeing you get depressed when you think about not spending time with me, but what I really do it for is to see your smile shine that much brighter afterwards." After finishing his explanation he looked directly at her. She tried to hold her smile back but she wasn't able to manage it for very long. "That's what I wanted to see."

Katerina punched him in the arm. "Let's get going." She was in a pretty good mood now. It was probably the best mood Theron had seen her in while going to the doctor's office, so at least he had made her happy enough to temporarily forget whatever was going on between her and Doctor Vaashti. Katerina knocked on the doctor's door. There was a longer pause than normal before they were given permission to enter.

When they opened the door they saw Deacon in the room with Doctor Vaashti. "Ah, speak of the devil," Deacon said as Theron entered the room behind Katerina.

"What's going on?" Theron asked.

"Oh, I was just informing the doctor that you would be asked to join the Student Council as the special scholarship student, and that you would no longer be able to report to her every day as a health officer," Deacon explained.

"And I'm trying to tell him that it's not just because you're a health officer that you need to come every day. I'm still working on trying to figure out if you have any underlying health issues that could have caused your coma," Doctor Vaashti retorted.

"And how long will that take? Have you made any progress?" Deacon questioned the doctor. "You can't just keep someone on daily observation indefinitely when there are no indications of a possible relapse. If you must keep him under observation at all then you should reduce it to a weekly schedule, rather than daily."

The doctor glared at Deacon before she responded, "I suppose you have a point, but I still want him to continue his health officer duties when he is able and to attend the weekly meetings every Saturday. I'll stop asking that he report to me every day though."

Deacon nodded. "That will be fine. Theron, I was going to look for you after I finished up here, so it's good that you came. I have some reports that should catch you up on everything you need to know about the Student Council. Please go over them sometime today. Starting tomorrow I want you to report to the Student Council offices after lunch."

Theron had expected this to happen eventually, but he didn't think it would be quite so soon. He remembered the chairwoman saying that she or Deacon would intervene and have him join the Student Council. At the time he wanted nothing more than to get away from the psychic vampire, but now he felt a pang of regret. Still, it wasn't like they were cutting contact completely. Theron took the papers from Deacon. "All right, I'll look them over tonight."

"Theron is going to be joining the Student Council?" Katerina sounded shocked. "I guess I shouldn't be surprised since he's the special scholarship student, but this is so sudden."

"Actually, he was supposed to be a member from the first day of school, but due to the incident we allowed Doctor Vaashti to have her way for a while," Deacon clarified. "However, we think it has been long enough. If the doctor keeps Theron any longer than this, we could see it as an abuse of her authority." Then Deacon grinned at Katerina. "Why? Did you want to join the council with him?"

"Could I?" Katerina asked hopefully.

"Nope, I'm afraid not." Deacon casually dashed her hopes. "Theron is a special case for this year. Everyone else who wants to be a member has to be elected normally, and even Theron will have to run for office if he wants to be a member next year." He seemed to enjoy watching Katerina grimace. "Anyway, my business here is done, so I'll take my leave." Deacon then walked out the door.

"Don't worry too much about it Katerina. You'll still be able to see me plenty." Theron patted Katerina on the head, trying to cheer her up.

"I think you two already spend too much time together as it is," Doctor Vaashti commented, clearly in a bad mood. "Actually, Miss Aikia, are you feeling well. I've been noticing over the past few days that you seem to be getting paler. Perhaps you should get more rest rather than chasing after Mr. Zeyla all the time."

"It's not like she's being a bother, Doctor Vaashti." Theron turned to Katerina again. "But now that she mentions it, you do look a little paler than when we first met. I guess I've spent so much time with you I haven't noticed the gradual change."

Katerina shot a glare at Doctor Vaashti. Apparently she didn't like having her condition exposed to Theron. "I'm fine. I've just been feeling a little tired lately with all the extra studying I've been doing. You don't need to worry about me Theron. I'll be fine for a few more weeks. I'll make sure I get plenty of rest over our extended break coming up."

"All right, but if you need to take a break it's okay. You're already doing really well in class, so it's not like you'll fall behind if you miss a day or two of studying," Theron said, concerned.

"You really shouldn't take such matters so lightly. Fatigue leaves you more susceptible to more severe health complications and makes your recovery slower," Doctor Vaashti counseled. "Anyway, you should take this chance to get some rest Miss Aikia."

"I said I'm fine. I'll get some rest later." Katerina was being stubborn, and she grabbed hold of Theron's arm, making it clear she wasn't leaving him.

Doctor Vaashti's eyes narrowed. "Have it your way. Now, Mr. Zeyla, I was finally able to finish gathering your medical records." The doctor pulled out a file from her desk and began flipping through the contents. "Everything appears pretty much as you had told me. In your infancy you had an extremely weak body. There was no explanation behind how you managed to survive, much less progress to the point that you were considered in above average health. By the time you got to elementary school and had annual physicals you were not only abnormally healthy, but your athletic capabilities were the top in your class."

Doctor Vaashti paused at this point and looked up from the file. "It appears unexplained and miraculous recoveries aren't new to you after all. Perhaps it isn't the reason you went into a coma that I should focus on, but how you came out of it." The doctor looked back to the file. "Everything else, though extraordinary, isn't of particular interest to me at the moment until I near the end of your file. It says you had a full blood workup trying to find out if you had contracted a wasting disease from your parents. I want you to tell me about that."

Theron was silent for a moment before slowly responding, "My parents died of the wasting disease you just mentioned. Apparently they had contracted it around the time I was four, but it hadn't been diagnosed as an unknown wasting disease until I was about seven. By the time I was eight it had become debilitating. The doctors tested me too in hopes that I might have developed an antibody for the disease since I showed no symptoms. At the very least, maybe the differences between my blood and theirs would have been able to help them isolate and identify the specific cause of the problem. In the end it didn't matter. No matter how many tests they ran, they never found anything that could help them cure my parents. They finally died two years later, shortly after I turned ten. At the funeral I heard so many comments about how unfortunate it was that while I was born weak and grew stronger, my parents were once perfectly healthy but withered away. For a while it made me think it was my fault they died, but as grew older I realized that was survivor's guilt."

Doctor Vaashti got out of her chair and put her hand on Theron's shoulder, looking him in the eye. "I'm sorry to hear that. You couldn't help it. You were simply too young and inexperienced to do anything about it."

Even Katerina put her hand on Theron's other shoulder and put her forehead on his back. She knew his parents were dead, but she still hadn't heard the specifics on how they had died. Theron let their sympathy sink into him. He had been pitied plenty, but it had always lacked the compassion and caring for his well-being that these two were showing. "Thanks, both of you. I'm all right now though. It's been a long time, and I'm finally starting to get my life back together."

Doctor Vaashti dropped her hand, but still held Theron with her eyes. "Just remember that you can come to me for help if you need it. I can't help feeling that if I had been around when your parents were sick I could have helped them. Anyway, I guess this will be the end of our daily meetings. I probably won't see you again until Saturday."

Theron nodded. "Yeah, I'll see you then Doctor Vaashti."

"Oh, one other thing. Since your daily visits are coming to an end, and in the future your visits will probably be more casual, why don't you call me Trish, at least when we're not doing anything official," Doctor Vaashti said. It caught Theron by surprise, and he could also feel Katerina tensing up. He guessed that maybe the doctor's sympathy had caused her to want to connect more with him, so she wanted to get rid of some of the professional distance they had both been maintaining.

Theron didn't want to upset Katerina too much, but he was actually happy about the doctor's request. "I'll think about it," Theron replied, trying to spare Katerina's feelings more than anything else. Even though she seemed okay around their classmates, Katerina really didn't like seeing him get closer than casual friendship with other people. Still, just calling Trish by her name shouldn't be such a big deal as long as he didn't appear too eager.

Trish smiled at him, seeming to guess what he was thinking. She probably hadn't missed Katerina's tension either. "That's fine. I'll see you two later. I assume Miss Aikia won't be coming back every day either."

"No, I guess I won't be," Katerina said stiffly. "We'll see you Saturday, Doctor Vaashti." Katerina gently tugged Theron towards the door.

Theron turned his head back as he followed Katerina. "Have a good day."

Once they were outside the door Katerina finally let Theron go, though she still seemed in a pretty bad mood. "I really don't like that woman."

"Well, at least you won't have to accompany me to see her every day now," Theron said with a shrug. He really didn't know what else he could say. "Anyway, I have another meeting to go to with the chairwoman. After that I'll meet up with Vincent so he can observe my athletic abilities. How about I call you when I'm done?"

Katerina started to pout. "It feels like we're having less and less time together."

Theron hadn't seen that expression in a while. "That

might be true, but we can't really expect to spend all of our time together. Don't worry, though. We'll make up for lost time over our break at your parents' place, right?" He hoped reminding her of their short vacation would cheer her up, and it did seem to help some.

"Yeah, I guess so, but you still better call me later," Katerina said, trying to hold him with her stare.

Even after being with her for most of his waking hours since he met her, Theron still found Katerina cute, but her stare wasn't as compelling as the one he had felt from Trish, not that he would ever dare bring that up with Katerina. He also wouldn't dare mention that he felt a strong connection to Trish that was very similar to the connection he felt to Katerina. All he could do was try to hide that from her and do his best to keep her smiling. No matter what, Katerina still had the best smile. "Don't worry; I'll definitely call you, so why don't you get some rest till then."

Katerina nodded. "Okay, I'll talk to you later then," she said as she started heading back to the female dormitory.

After Katerina was out of sight, Theron thought back on his meeting with Trish as he started walking towards the chairwoman's office. Three things stood out to him. The first was his disappointment that he wouldn't see her as often. The second was a small shock at how fast he had changed the way he addressed her in his thoughts, as if he'd wanted to call her Trish for a long time, but couldn't while he was maintaining their professional distance. The third was even more troubling. He was happy that he was getting closer to her. Two weeks ago he had been so afraid of her, but now he'd gone beyond being comfortable with being near her. Without really meaning to he was starting to like her, maybe even trust her a little bit. Even though she was a psychic vampire, not to mention a murderess,

Theron was starting to feel closer to her than he felt towards most humans, except Katerina of course.

His feelings were starting to get too out of control. He needed to ask for Uma's advice, but he'd have to be careful about it. He couldn't just tell the chairwoman everything. It would seem like a betrayal of her kindness towards him.

Theron's conflicted thoughts continued as he got on the elevator to ride up to Uma's office. He knocked on her door and waited for her permission before he entered. Uma had already rolled out a mat for him to sit on while he trained his abilities. Before he walked over to it though, he decided to voice his concerns. "Uma, before we begin, I need to talk to you."

"Oh, is it about Deacon getting you out of those daily observation sessions?" Uma asked.

"Indirectly," Theron admitted. "It's more like the feelings I'm experiencing are giving me some doubts."

Uma sighed. "I was afraid that might happen. That's why I tried to get you out as soon as I could. If we had waited much longer if may have been too late."

"What do you mean?" Theron asked.

Uma hesitated before explaining, "I didn't know for sure until now, but there was some evidence that indicated psychic vampires might have the ability to influence people's emotions. You see, more intense emotions create greater and purer amounts of the energy they feed on, so over time the psychic vampires learned to lace small amounts of energy with emotional charges and inject them into other people. This would intensify the emotions of those people, and in some cases implant whole new emotions. It seems likely the doctor has been feeding you a feeling of trust, and maybe even attraction. I wish I would have known about it sooner, but hopefully we got you out in time."

Hearing Uma's explanation threw Theron's thoughts

concerning Trish into chaos. How could he trust any of his feelings after hearing that? At the same time, it made sense to Theron. He wasn't the type to trust other's so quickly. Maybe the psychic vampire really had done something to influence him. That would explain why he had gotten so close to her. It wasn't like she had pursued him and shown him so much genuine affection like Katerina had. His feelings had been guiding his desire to draw closer to the doctor.

Theron slowly started to feel anger simmering within his heart. "Thanks for telling me, Uma. I wish I'd known that sooner. I think it would have helped keep her manipulations from affecting me, but why couldn't I sense it? I was able to feel her attack on that first night."

"I'm sorry I didn't warn you of the possibility," Uma apologized. "As for why you couldn't sense it, I imagine the amount of energy required to suddenly affect your memories would be much greater than slowly sculpting your emotions over time. Your training hasn't progressed enough yet to be able to sense small amounts of energy, but we'll start working on that today. You've already progressed remarkably well in the conscious control of your own energy."

Theron nodded. Conscious control of one's energy was actually simple. A person's energy, which went by several names including life energy, vital energy, or pranic energy, was stored within blood. It was responsive to the electrochemical impulses in the body meaning any nerve impulse or muscle movement would affect and expend a portion of a person's energy. This meant everyone constantly leaked out a small amount of energy that got released into the environment. Once the excess was released it was usually called ambient energy, and the amount released could be increased by periods of increased physical activity. Adding what Theron had just learned, it also indicated that life energy could be charged and purified with intense emotions.

That relationship between a person's energy and the physical body meant a person could gain conscious control over that constant flow of energy with practice. For the past few weeks Theron had been working on being able to quickly release and direct his energy to produce different results. So far, he had managed things like boiling water by exciting molecules with energy, and even cooling objects by pulling heat energy out of them. He could also cause electricity to arc through air by using his own energy to fill gaps in incomplete circuits.

That experiment had led Theron to ask Uma if he could use electricity to recharge his own energy, but she had laughed at the thought and told him he couldn't. Apparently just because different forms of energy could interact with each other didn't mean they were interchangeable. For example, even though Theron could use his energy to link electricity from one point to another and create a circuit, he couldn't use his energy to power a device that required electricity. The only way he could regain his energy was through rest, or draining it from another living thing, but Theron couldn't see how he'd be any different than the psychic vampire he was training to fight if he took his energy from other people.

During the course of his training so far, Theron had learned to clearly see the energy he was consciously directing, but he was dealing with rather large quantities, and as Uma had said, he hadn't learned to sense smaller amounts of energy yet. Now that was about to change. He sat down on the mat in a full lotus position, each foot resting on top of the thigh of the opposite leg. Uma had been teaching him to access his energy through his chakras, the key meeting points of energy within the body. They weren't actually physical, but existed as part of the overall network of energy within a person called the energy body or subtle body. Theron cleared his mind and began feeling the energy pooling at those points.

"Today, I don't want you to try to direct your energy consciously. Instead, I want you to focus on feeling your energy," Uma instructed. "Feel what your body is doing with your energy beyond your direction. Just like your physical body draws a breath when it needs air, your energy body also seeks out energy when it feels itself running low. In many cases this may come across as a form of hunger, and some people try to fill it with physical food, but as I explained to you before, you can't substitute one kind of energy for another. The kind of energy in food is also necessary, but fundamentally different than the energy of the energy body. If a person grows in understanding of his or her energy body, that person will come to be able to differentiate between the hunger for life energy and a hunger for food."

"I think I know what you mean," Theron responded in a relaxed tone. "I feel so drained after these sessions, and it starts to feel like my stomach is empty. At first I did think it was hunger, but it didn't really make sense because I eat lunch before coming here. As I thought about what you taught me, I realized that what I was feeling was my energy being depleted. I reasoned that, because a lot of energy pools in the navel chakra, emptying it of energy would make my brain think my stomach was empty due to their proximity."

"That's correct. You did well realizing that," Uma complimented. "However, you should also realize that once you've learned how to control energy, your subconscious will begin acting out with it as well. As I said, your energy body will also seek out energy when it feels itself running low. Before your training, that would simply be expressing itself in tiredness and hunger. Over time you would rest and the energy would start to replenish itself, and the feeling would pass. Now that you've learned to send your energy out, your energy body has new options open to it. You may begin to subconsciously drain life energy from others. That's why it is absolutely necessary you have an accurate picture of what your own energy is doing. If you only focus on what you are consciously controlling you could endanger others, especially after an intense energy workout."

Theron paused, thinking about Katerina. Could the fact that she was getting more tired lately be because he was draining her life energy without being aware of it? If that was true then he really did need to hurry and master becoming fully aware of his energy so he could bring it under control, but what could he do in the mean time? "How could I minimize the danger to others until I can learn to gain control over that?"

Uma smiled, though Theron couldn't see it. "If you consciously feed on multiple people it will put less stress on a single individual. Once your need is met your energy body won't demand more, so your subconscious shouldn't feed on its own."

Theron didn't have much of a choice. Apparently he was going to end up feeding on people regardless. In order to protect a small number of people from being fed on too much he'd have to consciously feed on more people to minimize the damage he was doing. "How does that make me any different than a psychic vampire?" Theron asked, getting depressed.

"It may not make you much different in terms of needing to feed on energy, but what you do with your abilities can set you worlds apart from them. Rather than murdering and using your abilities for selfish manipulations, you could learn to influence people's emotions and thoughts to bring peace to warring nations, or prevent corruption. You could directly intervene in any number of ways. One day you could probably come to rule the world, and make sure everyone adored you." Uma bent over and hugged Theron. "Just like I adore you."

Theron smiled at her. She always complimented him and seemed to like coming into contact with him, yet at the same time she never seemed to come across as romantically affectionate. It always felt more like a mother to him for some reason, and this really wasn't any different. "I don't know about ruling the world, but bringing peace and preventing corruption do sound like good ideas. First I need to get this down though." Theron closed his eyes and felt Uma release him.

Theron tried to merge his consciousness with his energy body, trying to feel it as he felt his physical body. Slowly his physical body started growing numb and distant. The feeling scared him and he stopped, snapping his consciousness back. Everything seemed normal, and he had full sensation again as if nothing had happened. He started drifting away again, this time allowing the numbness to envelope him. After he couldn't feel his body anymore, he began to notice what he could only describe as a faint tingling sensation spreading out from him. He couldn't think very well, as if his mind, body and soul had all become detached from one another, and he was drifting between them. He wasn't aware of anything beyond that.

Theron began trying to approach his mind, but a force seemed to stop him. He was filled with a feeling and a single thought that exploded in what was left of his consciousness. The feeling and the thought were two parts of the same message: he wasn't ready. He tried asking what he wasn't ready for, but he was answered with silence. This time he decided to try to move towards his soul. There was no resistance this time as his sense of self merged with his soul, and he could feel he was in a form. It wasn't like the physical body. He couldn't feel heat or cold, or any air from the heater that had gently stirred the hairs on his arms only a few moments ago.

This body felt more self-contained, but at the same time it felt free from any constraints. He could feel a sensation that reminded him of water flowing through a pipe, causing a fast paced vibration and a faint humming sound. Theron tried to open his eyes, but his eyelids wouldn't move. However, he suddenly became aware. It wasn't like normal sight, but he didn't know how else to describe it. He could see everything in a full circle around him. He didn't look, but instead simply focused his attention on his body. He could see his own aura and the pulse of energy through his veins. He could make out the pools of energy where his chakras were. He lifted the arm of his energy body. His physical arm remained behind and he viewed his arm in its pure energy state.

Viewing his energy this was made it look grander than he thought it would, and Theron became intimately aware with the fact that the energy body was another name for the soul. The energy body was eternal. Even if his physical body perished, his energy would continue to exist. Feeling and seeing his energy body as he did now made Theron certain of that. His physical body was necessary to interact with the world, but in a sense it was only a tool. The energy body, the soul, was what really mattered.

The thoughts scared Theron. He didn't doubt they were true, but they were so alien to everything he had known before. His fear forced him to focus on what he could see, rather than think about what it meant. The first thing that drew Theron's attention was what appeared to be a chain extending out from his soul. Through the chain he could feel emotions and a small trace of life energy. Theron realized it was connected to another person, but he couldn't figure out who might be at the other end. He also noticed little tendrils of energy spreading out from him. They seemed to be reaching out and absorbing small bits of the ambient energy around him. For some reason, he couldn't really make out what Uma's energy looked like. It seemed to be wrapped up in itself, not emitting anything that could be viewed, so it appeared like nothingness. It vaguely reminded Theron of what he imagined a black hole would be like.

After he was done looking around he tried to pull himself back into his physical body, but he was having trouble doing it for some reason. He tried letting his awareness slip away, but he was having trouble shutting it off. He already knew he couldn't move his physical body as he normally would, so as a last resort he tried using his energy to directly affect his physical nervous system. He was aware that his physical arm started to spasm. Seeing that, Uma came over.

"What's wrong Theron?" Uma waited for a response, but Theron couldn't answer. "Hold on, you may have meditated too deeply. It can happen sometimes when you're inexperienced. In the future, if you keep your eyes open it'll be easier to come back since vision is usually the most dominant sense. Of course it'll be harder to get into a trance with your eyes opened. Anyway, I'll try to use some smelling salts. The sense of smell can also be pretty powerful, so this should jolt you out." Uma pulled out a packet and broke it open under Theron's nose. The overpowering smell jolted him back into his physical body.

"Oh god that smells awful," Theron complained. "But thanks Uma. I guess that's what they call an out of body experience, but I had no idea it was so hard to get back into your physical body."

"Not quite," Uma clarified. "What you actually experienced was a transferring of your consciousness from your physical body to your soul. In an out of body experience, your consciousness is projected out, but it actually separated from your soul which remains in your physical body. Because of that fact, you remain anchored during an out of body experience, making it much easier to return from.

"A consciousness transfer is a completely different matter because you're not projecting your consciousness outward. Instead you are withdrawing to a deeper part of yourself. When you do that, your energy body has a stronger hold on you than your physical body because the flesh is basically just a shell at that point. Returning from it is very difficult without practice. What you did can actually be quite dangerous. I didn't expect you to go that far. How deep you go into your energy body is mostly determined by your starting point when you switch over. I'm guessing you waited till you completely lost all physical sensation before transferring your consciousness." Theron nodded to confirm Uma's suspicion.

"I should have foreseen that." Uma sighed. "You have to be as close to the border between the two as you can so that a subtle shift of focus from your physical body to your energy body will be enough to transfer your consciousness. To do that, you want to be able to suppress your physical awareness just barely enough to begin to feel your energy body, so you're feeling a little of both at the same time. Now that you have some experience you'll be able to recognize that line much easier. More importantly though, were you able to open your third eye?"

"My third eye?" Theron questioned. "I thought it was just a chakra point, but is that what was causing that complete awareness I had? It wasn't quite like seeing with my eyes, but I could visualize everything around me, including my energy body."

"Yes, that's it. It's also known as the mind's eye. If you can recall the sensation of opening it you'll be able to see the flow of energy without having to send your consciousness all the way into your energy body," Uma explained.

"I think I can do that. I'll make that my homework project," Theron responded as he got up.

"That sounds like a good idea. You really are a fast learner." Uma favored Theron with another smile.

"Thanks. I'll see you again tomorrow Uma," Theron said as he headed out of her office. Theron still had to talk to Vincent and then call Katerina, but he had managed to figure out what was going on with his feelings regarding Trish, and he had taken a big step forward on the next phase of his training. All said, it'd been a pretty good day already.

* * * * *

After Theron had left her office, the chairwoman headed over to her phone. She immediately dialed a number on it and waited for the other side to pick up. "Hello, Deacon. It seems our little pet project was starting to harbor doubts about going against Trish Vaashti. I dealt with it for now, but we should arrange another incident to make sure he stays on the path we want him on."

Deacon's voice came back over the phone. "May I suggest we wait until after the athletic competition, my lady? We don't want to arrange it so soon after he expressed those doubts. It would be a little too convenient."

"That's fine," the chairwoman consented. "We've cut down on the contact between those two anyway, so we should have a bit more time. I'll leave the details to you."

"As you wish, my lady." The chairwoman heard a click from the other side and she hung up the phone. She picked up a cup of tea. It had already gone cold. The chairwoman stared at the cup for a few moments until it started to steam faintly, then took a sip. Soon she'd have to start showing her hand. She just hoped she had planted enough seeds in Theron. She truly thought she might regret it if she had to kill him.

Chapter 5

Wrongs Made Right

Theron sat in a train car watching the scenery go by. Katerina was resting her head on his shoulder as she slept. The past few weeks since Theron had joined the Student Council had gone by in a flash. After his classes in the morning, he had typically been spending his afternoons in the council offices, learning the procedures of the council and trying to figure out where he could best fit in. Deacon acted as laid-back as ever, so Theron usually ended up going to the vice-president whenever he had any problems.

Theron and Adrasteia worked well together, but every now and then Deacon would say or do something to stir things up. It turned out the vice-president's biggest responsibility was to keep the president in line and make sure he did his job, to which Deacon would respond that his most important job was to be admired by the students. Still, the balance between the president and vice-president seemed to keep things fun, and, despite his carefree attitude, Deacon did do a lot of work coordinating with the event committee and negotiating a lot of things with faculty and staff members. The Student Council had at least a say, and usually the final decision, on just about everything on campus. Their power was immense, and their enormous responsibilities kept them busy.

Theron had also been continuing his psychic training with Uma. He hadn't tried transferring his consciousness into his energy body again, but he had managed to make progress opening his third eye. He couldn't see the chain extending from his energy body he had seen when he had transferred his consciousness, but when he had asked Uma about it she explained the reason he couldn't see it with just normal viewing was probably because it was connected to his energy body on a very deep level.

After Theron was able to comfortably expand his awareness with his third eye he had tried using it during a health officer meeting. He was able to detect every layer of the other students' auras, extending out from their energy bodies like a mist, with perfect clarity. Using his normal eyes, Theron would only be able to see a few of the layers closer to the core of the body when the lighting was just right.

When he focused on Trish though, he was shocked by the density of her energy. The particles of energy radiating from Trish looked more like a wave than mist. However, in spite of the density, the aura didn't seem as clear to Theron as the students had been. It looked distorted, like something viewed through the heat of a flame. Theron realized Trish must be concealing her energy somehow which gave it the distorted effect. Otherwise, the density would have made it clearly visible to anyone, and that would give her inhuman nature away.

Theron had also been careful to not feed on anyone in Trish's presence since he assumed she would already be able to see his energy in the same way he was just learning to see hers. However, he had started consciously feeding on small amounts of the life energy of just about everyone he passed by. Spreading out his feeding among as many people as possible seemed to be working. Looking at Katerina resting on his shoulder now, Theron could see she was looking much less pale than she did a couple weeks ago. In fact, she had been so energetic with excitement about their trip to her parents' house that she had come knocking on the door to his room at six o'clock that morning, telling him to get ready in a hurry because the train would be leaving.

Theron had gotten ready and they made it to the station in time for the six forty-five departure. It had taken them about two hours to get to Salzburg, Austria from the campus. From there they switched to a train heading for Munich, Germany, and about two more hours later they had to switch trains again to get to Berlin. During that time, Katerina had talked excitedly about what her home was like and made plans about what they could do while they were there.

Eventually her excitement had given way to weariness and she fell asleep shortly after they boarded the train to Berlin. She had admitted that she hadn't slept the night before, so Theron was glad to see her resting. He was happy that she was recovering from the effect of his inadvertent draining of her energy. Her recovery helped alleviate some of his guilt.

They had been on their current train for almost six hours, and an announcement had been made that they were about fifteen minutes from their destination. Katerina was still sleeping, and Theron couldn't bring himself to shake her awake, so he gently called out to her. "Katerina, we're almost there. You need to wake up now."

She didn't show any sign of waking up, so he started tickling her ear and gently playing with her hair. She tried to brush away his hand, but as she did he took hold of her hand. The motion made her look even more adorable, but Theron really needed to get her awake, so he continued to tickle her ear as he held on to her hand. At first she scrunched her face and shook her head, but shortly after she opened her eyes.

It took her a few moments to get her bearings, but once she did Katerina blushed and looked up into Theron's eyes. He let go of her hand and gave the explanation her eyes silently cried out for. "Good evening, Katerina. Sorry to wake you up, but we're almost to Berlin. I didn't want to just shake you awake, so I tried calling out to you first. Since that didn't work, I tried to wake you up as gently as I could. You can be a pretty persistent sleeper."

Katerina's blush deepened another shade as she sat up straight. "I'm sorry, your shoulder must be tired."

"It's fine. I just hope you were comfortable." Theron smiled at her. "As soon as you're ready, we should probably gather our things so we can get off the train. Where are we going from here?"

"There should be a car waiting for us outside the station. My parents' house is in Lichterfelde West, so it'll take about twenty minutes to get there," Katerina answered.

"All right." Theron nodded. He gathered his and Katerina's luggage stowed in the racks above their heads. Soon after, the train came to a stop and all the passengers began to disembark.

Theron paused and looked around in awe as he got off the train. The station was enormous. There were so many people around that he was finding it difficult to breathe, but at the same time seeing so much life in one place made him excited.

Katerina couldn't grab his hand since he was holding their luggage, so she looped her arm through his to make sure they didn't get separated. In spite of all the activity, the station wasn't particularly loud. Katerina didn't even have to raise her voice for Theron to hear her. "I've heard that this station serves about three hundred thousand people each day with about sixteen hundred trains. It was pretty overwhelming my first couple of times, but you get used to it. Just stay close to me."

Katerina led Theron away from the train. Apparently they were on a subterranean level of the station. Theron hadn't noticed it at first because the station's architecture let sunlight filter down even to the lowest levels. It wasn't until Katerina guided him up a flight of stairs that he realized they had been underground.

Katerina continued to lead him until she seemed to see someone she recognized. She walked towards a man and called, "Varick, we're here."

The man turned towards Katerina and bowed to her. "Welcome back, my lady. I suppose this is the friend you spoke of." Varick eyed Theron, but after a short inspection nodded in approval. "It's good to see someone with proper manners, carrying a lady's luggage for her. You may call me Varick. I have been in service to the Schicksal family since before the young lady was born."

"Schicksal family?" Theron questioned.

"Oh, I forgot that I never told you. That's my real family name," Katerina explained. "My parents chose it when they were married. My mother is German and my father is Russian. Since Germany and Russia have different traditions for surnames, they decided to break from both traditions and pick a whole new name. Mother told me they picked Schicksal because they felt like their meeting and falling in love was fate."

"That sounds pretty romantic," Theron commented.

"Indeed, their love is like a modern Romeo and

Juliet, without the tragic ending," Varick added. "Those two developed a deep love for each other during their time as diplomats, but they served opposing interests. Master Adrik was a member of the Russian diplomatic mission to West Germany before the fall of the Berlin Wall. Lady Maria was a part of the under-secretary of state's staff and is related to the old Prussian royalty. When they decided to get married, their union was strongly opposed by their respective governments, but they fought to be together. Lady Maria resigned from her position in the government, and Master Adrik was demoted to a cultural attaché, but due to lessening tensions and his own good relations with his superiors, he was ultimately allowed to remain in Germany. Now they've become a symbol of hope for ever closer relations between the peoples of Germany and Russia."

"Well, now that you know my family history, maybe we can get going," Katerina said, breaking back into the conversation. "If you let him, Varick will go on about my parents until night fall."

Varick chuckled. "Yes, I'm sorry, my lady. Still, I wouldn't have to go on like this if you had told him yourself."

"We're not really supposed to talk about our private lives at school," Katerina replied, but then added in a quieter tone. "Besides, it's embarrassing talking about my parents like that."

"Well, you already know some things about me, so I guess we're even now," Theron said with a smile.

Katerina looked at him and grinned before nodding. "I guess we are."

Varick led Theron and Katerina to a limousine in the underground parking area. He opened the trunk and stowed the luggage Theron had been carrying. Theron and Katerina got into the back and Varick started to drive. Theron spent most of the trip looking out the window. Every now and then he thought he might have vaguely recognized some of the buildings. Those recognitions grew more frequent once they arrived in the Lichterfelde West.

"I think I've been here before," Theron commented.

"Well, you did say you were born in Berlin, maybe you came with your parents?" Katerina asked.

Theron nodded. "I must have. The orphanage is in Bonn, almost four hundred miles away. I know I lived in Berlin before that, but I can't remember where exactly. I feel like I should remember where I spent the first ten years of my life, but to be honest, I didn't leave my house very often when I was growing up. Between me being weak when I was young and my parents growing ill when I was older, I didn't really go out too much. There were a few years in between when my parents would take me out to parties, but I never really paid attention to where we went. Come to think of it, since my parents were also diplomats, I wonder if they knew your parents."

Katerina seemed thoughtful. "It's possible. Why don't you ask my parents?"

"I think I will." Theron nodded. The two sat in silence the rest of the way. Lichterfelde West was filled with villas and mansions. It was obvious that anyone living there would be fairly well off. A thought that only made Theron more sure that he and his parents had once lived there.

After a few more minutes Varick stopped the limousine in front of a large villa with a circle driveway. He got out of the driver's seat and came around to open the door for Theron and Katerina. The two got out and walked to the door. A maid came to the entrance before they could knock and opened the door for them.

"Thank you, Ancilla." Katerina nodded at the maid.

"Welcome home, Lady Katerina." The maid curtsied. "Dinner is about to be served. Master Adrik asked me to direct you there at your earliest convenience."

"I need to freshen up first. Could you wait here with Theron?" Katerina asked as she started walking away.

"Of course, my lady," Ancilla answered before turning to Theron. "Do you need anything before dinner, sir?"

"I'm all right, thank you," Theron replied. He wasn't used to being waited on. It felt a little uncomfortable to him. He and the maid just stood there for a few minutes waiting for Katerina to return. Theron felt relieved when she finally came back.

"Sorry to keep you waiting. Are you ready to meet my parents?" Katerina asked Theron.

"No, actually I'm starting to get really nervous, but there's no point in putting it off," Theron answered.

"It'll be fine. Though come to think of it, I only asked them if I could bring a friend over. I never said you were a boy. Oh well, my father wouldn't kill you, probably," Katerina commented with a grin.

"That's such a comforting thought, thank you so much Katerina," Theron responded sarcastically.

The two followed the maid, Ancilla, through the house until they entered a large formal dining room. There were several servants standing on the side of the room. A man and a woman were seated at the table. They stood up when they saw Theron and Katerina enter.

The woman, who must have been Maria, greeted them first. "Katerina, welcome home dear. I trust the new term at school is going well. It's the first time you've brought over a friend, so you must be starting to enjoy it some."

"I have been enjoying this year so far, in large part due to meeting this boy." Katerina indicated Theron.

Theron stepped forward and bowed to Katerina's parents. Her father, Adrik, had been looking at Theron since he entered, and Theron decided to direct his greeting directly towards him. "Greetings to you both. My name is Theron Zeyla. I—" Theron's introduction was interrupted by a clattering sound behind him.

Varick had entered the room carrying place settings for Theron and Katerina, but had dropped them. Varick was frozen in place, staring at Theron. As Theron looked around he noticed that Maria's eyes had widened in shock and Adrik's face was turning red.

Katerina's father quickly walked over to Theron and grabbed him by the collar. "You! How dare you come here now! What sick game are you playing? Wasn't it enough that you broke my daughter's heart once?" Adrik was practically roaring at Theron.

"What are you talking about?" Theron grabbed hold of Adrik's hand to stabilize himself against the pressure Adrik was applying. "I have never hurt Katerina, and I would never do so willingly." Theron looked Katerina's father directly in the eyes in an attempt to show his sincerity.

Adrik only seemed to grow more furious. "Liar. If you knew how much we wanted to bring you into our home, you would never make such a claim. You spat on our kindness, and on the memory of your mother and father!"

The words shocked Theron. "You knew my parents? Tell me, what did I do? What are you so angry about? I don't remember seeing you before, and I just met Katerina a little over a month ago."

Maria came up beside her husband and placed her hand on his shoulder, calming him enough for him to release Theron. "I'm not surprised that you don't remember us, we spent most of our time at your house with your parents, but you mean you don't remember Katerina as well? You were playmates for years."

Katerina had been in shock at her father's outburst, but was finally recovering enough to come up beside Theron. "What do you mean, mother?"

"So he isn't the only one not to recognize a dear friend," Maria said with a frown. "Katerina, this was the boy you played with as a child, the one we told you we were going to adopt, but then he decided to refuse us."

Katerina was struck speechless, but for Theron, everything seemed to fall into place. He remembered a theory Uma had told him when he had first met her. "You're the ones," Theron managed to say with his mind racing. "Please allow me to confirm something. Did my parents mean for you to take care of me after their death?"

Maria looked at Theron with a puzzled look. "Yes, I thought that had been made quite clear in your parents' will."

Theron could barely keep himself from laughing. The entire situation suddenly seemed so absurd. They had all been tricked, but now that they had met, they could learn the truth. Theron began to explain his side of the story to Katerina's parents. "The will I saw dictated that I should be given to an orphanage in Bonn."

Adrik scoffed, "That's impossible."

Theron shook his head. "No, I can assure you it isn't. I had hoped that one day I'd have a breakthrough in reclaiming my past, but I never expected it to come like this, and in such a short time. The executor of the will used my situation to craft a scheme that would allow him access to my parents' estate. He falsified a will that gave him the right to reimburse the orphanage for any expenses related to my upbringing. The headmaster in turn had padded those expenses in every possible way he could, and he split the profits with the executor. I only learned the true extent of their scheme about half a year ago, and it was only about a month ago that someone told me there was probably another party that might know what the original will should have been. The executor would have had to tell a lie to the people with whom my parents had made arrangements with for my care to insure they didn't try to claim me."

For the first time, Adrik seemed thoughtful. "That's a little hard to swallow, but I suppose it could be possible. If your story is true, I'll have the executor thrown in prison for a very long time. Let's call him here and find out. He still operates out of Berlin. I'll have him out here tonight."

"Given that I recently ran away from the orphanage to attend New Babel Academy, he may be worried that I contacted you. He may not be willing to come," Theron warned.

"I wasn't going to make it a request," Adrik said. There was a dangerous gleam in his eyes.

"While you're handling that dear, I'll take Theron and Katerina to another room. We should probably give Theron the benefit of the doubt until we verify his story." Maria turned to the servants. All of them looked very uncomfortable. "I'm sorry that you all had to witness that. I'm also sorry that we'll have to postpone dinner until this last minute business is concluded. You all may go about your normal tasks for the remainder of the day. I'll take care of our guest personally."

As Maria guided Theron and Katerina out of the room, Theron glanced back and saw Adrik giving instructions to Varick, then Theron followed Maria and Katerina to a smaller room that appeared to be a study. Maria went over to a filing cabinet and started going through it. After a few minutes, she came over to Theron holding a folded sheet of paper. "This is for you," Maria said, holding out the paper.

Theron took the paper and unfolded it. He read over the contents. "This is a copy of the original will, isn't it?"

"That's correct," Maria confirmed.

"Why would you agree to look after me?" Theron questioned. "And not just that, but according to this will you were going to adopt me as your own child, not just act as a guardian."

Maria smiled. "Your parents played a large role in getting our governments to accept Adrik and I getting married. They were wonderful people. We loved them as much as friends could love one another. Beyond that, Katerina was quite taken with you. She never was able to make friends before you, and hasn't really made any since."

"Mother!" Katerina exclaimed as she blushed.

"Well, you did say the boy from your childhood and I were the only people you ever felt a strong connection to," Theron recalled. "I should apologize though. Even if I didn't do it because of my own will, I see now that I did leave you alone. I did hurt you, just like your father said."

Katerina shook her head. "To be honest, it still hasn't sunk in yet, but learning that the boy I knew didn't really want to be separated from me makes me happy. Even though we've lost a lot of time, we did manage to meet again. Even though you were gone for a while, you didn't really leave me alone after all. You couldn't help what happened in the past, and you've promised to not leave me alone, so I'll believe in you."

"Good girl." Maria patted her daughter on the head. "Meaningful relationships take a lot of work, and require a lot of understanding and tolerance. I hope we can all work on our relationship as a family after today."

"I've been without a family for a long time. To be honest, I'm not sure how to act in one anymore, but I think I'd like to try," Theron said solemnly.

"It does sound like you've lived a hard life these past six years, but I think it's almost time for it to end. Should we go listen in on Adrik's interrogation of this corrupt executor?" Maria asked.

"I want to, besides, if he starts lying I want to be there to call him out on it," Theron answered.

Maria nodded with a small smile and guided Theron and Katerina to a door. She pushed the door open a crack, letting sound pass through. The three waited there until they finally heard people entering the room.

"What is the meaning of this? It's an outrage to demand that I come when it's not even business hours. Not only do you demand, but you even send a thug to ensure I comply. I'll see you sued for this." The voice was yelling beyond the door.

"I'm an attaché to a diplomatic mission. Good luck suing me, Mr. Jakob," Adrik's voice answered the other man's protest. "Besides, the matter I wish to speak with you about should have been settled years ago. I recently received some new information that suggests you may not have been honest with us regarding young Mr. Zeyla's decision to not be adopted by us. I would like for you to confirm the facts for me."

Mr. Jakob, the executor of the will Theron's parents had made, was silent for a moment. Theron pushed the door open a little further so he could see through the crack. The worried look on Mr. Jakob's face brought a small smile to Theron's lips.

Finally, Mr. Jakob responded to the accusation. "This is ridiculous. That happened six years ago. Why bring it up now? Theron Zeyla didn't want to be adopted. He was afraid it would dishonor his memory of his parents and be a betrayal of their love for him."

"Then let me hear the words from his own mouth," Adrik demanded in a firm tone.

"I'm afraid that's not possible," Mr. Jakob responded. "I heard that he recently fled the orphanage he had been entrusted to. I don't know where he is."

Maria gently pushed Theron from behind, indicating he should go out and join the conversation. Theron nodded to her and walked into the room. "I fled the orphanage because I learned what you and the headmaster were really doing," Theron stated.

Mr. Jakob turned pale when he saw Theron, but slowly his cheeks began to flush. "How dare you! After all the care we gave you for the past six years, this is how you repay us?"

"Care? You used caring for me as a pretense to siphon money from my parents' estate for your own personal gain." Theron pulled out the will that Maria had given him. "And now I find this. Another will very different from the one you showed me. I wonder which one would hold up in court."

"That will is older, only the most recent will needs to be enforced. Felecia and Renaud Zeyla changed their mind in their final days. They didn't trust the Schicksal family would be able to raise you." Mr. Jakob was starting to panic now.

"Oh, that's news to me," Adrik said. "I think Felecia and Renaud would have told us if they were having doubts. We were very close friends after all. Besides, that wasn't what you told us originally."

Now Maria entered the room. "This is getting

nowhere. I don't think Mr. Jakob will admit the truth even though he's obviously speaking from both sides of his mouth. It's apparent he's been telling Theron one thing and us another. We won't get the truth from him, so let us take this matter to court. We have our copy of the will. Let him produce his own copy. We'll then let everyone tell their side of the story and let the law settle this matter. I think it's clear which side justice will favor, and I believe the penalties for fraud with the false will and embezzlement from the Zeyla estate over the years will be quite harsh."

"Can't we work something out?" Mr. Jakob was clearly scared by Maria's proposition. "I'll help you draw up the paperwork to adopt Theron properly if you want, and I'll even try to give as much of the money back to the Zeyla estate as I can."

Theron walked up to Mr. Jakob. "That's fine, but before that, I want to hear the truth from you."

Mr. Jakob's fear finally loosened his tongue. "All right, just don't take me to court."

Theron nodded. "I won't take you to court."

Mr. Jakob looked a little relieved. "It's as you've guessed. The will the Schicksal family possesses is authentic. I was tired of distributing other people's wealth, and only getting scraps in return. I deserved more. So when I got involved with your case I realized I had an opportunity to finally get away from just serving others. I made another will and conspired with the headmaster of the orphanage I took you to. Together we decided to start earning what we were due. We were very careful. We even made sure not to charge too much for any single transaction because eventually you'd grow old enough to inherit the estate and you'd figure out what we had done, so we made each transaction look plausible.

"The only loose end was the real will your parents

had made. When they were still alive they had asked that I make a second copy and give it to the Schicksal family to get their agreement. Of course they did agree, and they kept the second copy, so I had to lie to them. I told the Schicksal family that you hated them and absolutely refused to live with them. I counseled them that in this case, it would be better for you if we didn't enforce the will, and that I'd find a suitable guardian for you. They accepted that solution, and I didn't have any problems until you suddenly ran away. In truth, I think I started suspecting something like this might happen since then."

"Varick, did you get all that?" Adrik asked.

Varick came into the room from another door. "Yes Master Adrik. I was able to record everything."

Adrik nodded in approval. "Good, please arrange for Mr. Jakob to be handed over to the authorities. I plan to see him rot in prison for a very long time for this. Maria. Theron. You both did well getting the truth from him."

"Wait, this isn't what we agreed! You promised I wouldn't be taken to court!" Mr. Jakob protested.

Adrik turned back towards Mr. Jakob. "Mr. Zeyla said he wouldn't take you to court, and he won't. I will. Do you honestly think an apology and paying back the money you stole would also make up for the time we lost? The pain we suffered? In truth, even if you rot in a cell for the rest of your life it wouldn't be enough, but at least it's something."

"No! I refuse to accept this!" Mr. Jakob turned to run, but he was immediately struck by Varick. The blow brought Mr. Jakob to his knees.

"Forgive me sir, but my master asked me to turn you over to the authorities, so I can't have you running away." Varick said in a tone full of satisfaction. He had been serving the Schicksal family long enough to know the pain Mr. Jakob's actions had caused, and he didn't hold back his wrath.

Adrik turned back to Theron. "Mr. Zeyla. No, Theron. I should apologize to you, both for my conduct earlier this evening, and for six years ago. I should have asked to hear from you directly back then. To be honest, it wasn't just my daughter's heart that was broken when we heard you really hated us. You wouldn't have known this, but Maria and I started watching you and Katerina playing together after your parents asked us if we would be willing to adopt you. Watching you two play together, Maria and I began to think about us as a family. We probably should have talked with you more back then, and let you know how we felt, but we didn't want to interfere with the remaining time you had with your parents. When Felecia and Renaud died, we grieved deeply for them, and when Mr. Jakob came during that vulnerable time and told us his lies we were so hurt we didn't even think to question them. If we had, we might have avoided all this tragedy. I'm sorry."

Theron shook his head. "You don't need to apologize. We were both victims. Besides, you chose to believe me even after you had suffered so much. I have so much to thank you for. I had thought resolving my situation would take years, but thanks to meeting Katerina again it was resolved in a month. I can't even imagine what the odds of this happening were."

Maria came up and hugged Theron. "It was never about odds. Katerina had often told me how she felt about you. I believe you two share a special connection that time and space could never sever. No matter what happens, you two will always be drawn back together." Maria then gave Theron a radiant smile. It was clear where Katerina had gotten her own smiles from. "You definitely deserve to be a Schicksal. Fate pulls at you. I know you probably won't be able to think of Adrik and I as your father and mother, but is it all right for us to think of you as our son?"

Theron's emotions had been tossed about all evening, but Maria's question finally settled them. A single tear worked its way down his cheek. Theron couldn't remember the last time he had really felt like he was home, but the warmth he felt now made him truly happy. "Of course you can," Theron answered Maria with a smile.

Katerina had been crying for the past few minutes. When she heard Theron's words she ran up and hugged her mother and Theron together. Even Adrik's eyes looked a little moist as he rested his hands on his family. His whole family.

Chapter 6

Game's End

Theron's eyes opened as he lay in the bed in his dorm room at New Babel Academy. He glanced at the clock on his nightstand. The time read five forty-five in the morning. His alarm would go off in about fifteen minutes. Rather than get up a little early, he decided to close his eyes and wait for the alarm. He thought back on the past few days.

Katerina's parents had cleared their schedules so they could spend time getting to know him and to help him deal with his circumstances. *I guess they're not just Katerina's parents anymore.* Theron corrected his thoughts. Part of their help had included formally adopting him, so they were his parents now too. That would take some getting used to. Adrik and Maria had been very kind to him through the whole process. They had even happily allowed him to keep his original family name, Zeyla. In fact, they had seemed surprised when he had asked if he could keep his name. They had never expected him to change it to match theirs. That gesture had reminded Theron how much the Schicksal family must have loved his mother and father.

Adrik and Maria had a surprising amount of influence. He had only been with them for a little over three days during the long weekend, but they had been able to finalize his adoption and have Mr. Jakob tried and convicted in that short time. They had even begun taking legal action against the headmaster of the orphanage for fraud against the Zeyla estate, but that process was made much more complicated by Theron's request to only sue him for the amount of the excess charges the headmaster had billed to his estate. Regardless of how it came about, it was still a fact that Theron had been taken care of in that orphanage. Theron didn't want the headmaster to serve time in prison. In fact, now that he had found a way out of the situation he had so despised, Theron was able to think more generously about his days in the orphanage. He was able to remember a few small kindnesses the headmaster had shown him, especially during the early days at the orphanage. More importantly, Theron didn't want any of the other children still living in the orphanage to suffer the consequences of the headmaster's actions,

In his anger during the past year, Theron had allowed himself to forgot about most of those things. It was easier to hate people if you demonized them by disregarding any positive aspects and reducing them to one-dimensional caricatures. But humans weren't that simple. In fact, most humans found justifications for their own actions that allowed them to continue to believe they were basically good people. Theron didn't know how the headmaster justified his own actions, and maybe the kindness he would occasionally show Theron was an act, but now that their situations were reversed and Theron was the one that had power over the headmaster's future, Theron wanted to be a better person. He didn't want to ruin the headmaster. Mr. Jakob would atone for what had been taken away from Theron, and that was enough.

His new parents had been shocked by Theron's request, but afterwards they smiled and agreed, mentioning that he really was the son of Felecia and Renaud. Maria and Adrik had spent almost every waking hour with Katerina and Theron over their break, allowing Varick to handle most of the details regarding the legal affairs. During the time they spent together, Theron usually asked about his new parents rather than talk about himself, and they obliged him. They seemed to adjust to the situation fairly quickly, and were considerate of his wish to avoid talking about his time in the orphanage.

On the other hand, it had taken Katerina a couple days for the reality to sink in and adjust her perspective. She had spent years thinking the boy she had felt so strongly about, her only real friend, had abandoned her. She had convinced herself that she was flawed in some way, so she had refused to get close to other people, afraid they would leave her too. Of course, she had gotten close to Theron anyway, but usually she was very careful not to do anything that might displease him.

Since their reunion a little over a month ago, Katerina had always been hesitant about making requests or doing anything that could be seen as selfish. She had only occasionally allowed herself to relax and assert her true self. Now that she had learned that the boy she had felt so strongly for didn't hate her, that they had simply been torn apart by a situation that was beyond their power to control, Katerina allowed herself to act much more spoiled. Katerina's selfish side made Theron remember the little girl he used to play with. In truth, if she had acted that way earlier, Theron probably would have recognized her. To say Katerina was pushy as a child was an understatement, but he had never minded her dragging him around. He had been rather isolated by his circumstances as a child, and she had pulled him out of that isolation when his parents had been too ill to do so themselves.

Of course, Adrik and Maria being with them had put a damper on things from Katerina's perspective. When she had voiced her opinion they told her she'd have plenty of time to spend with her new brother later, so Katerina should let them spend some time with Theron while they had a chance. Katerina's reaction had been to cling to Theron even more strongly when she had a chance. She had also started calling him "brother" occasionally.

The past few days had flown by so quickly that it surprised Theron. In the past, he had always enjoyed going to school, and during his time in the orphanage, school had become his refuge from his miserable life. However, yesterday when Theron had to get on the train to come back to school, he had felt a pang of sadness. That, more than anything else, spoke volumes about how Adrik and Maria made him feel. He wasn't a naturally trusting person, but in such a short period of time they had managed to find large places in his heart. He didn't want to part from them. Katerina on the other hand had seemed happy to get him all to herself again. She didn't talk much on their way back to the academy, but she had held his hand most of the trip, just enjoying being together.

When they had gotten back to the academy that night they remembered that they had totally forgotten to train themselves for the competition the next day, but there was nothing they could do about it. Theron wasn't really worried, but he had suggested they try to get to bed early so they could at least be as rested as possible. Katerina had reluctantly agreed. Before she'd left for her dormitory she kissed Theron on the cheek and wished him a good night. He had been a bit shocked at the time, but thinking back on it now he accepted it as a familial gesture from his new sister.

When he had gotten to his room, he'd looked up Uma's number. The chairwoman had given him the passcode to get in contact with her, and he had promised he would call her when he returned from his vacation. She picked up the phone right away. Theron gave her a brief summary of his time with the Schicksals, mostly focusing on the issue regarding the will.

The chairwoman had seemed glad for him, but she'd also expressed disappointment that the issue was resolved without her really doing anything. Theron had disagreed with her, pointing out the fact that he never would have met Katerina or her parents if Uma hadn't accepted him into the academy in the first place. Ultimately, the chairwoman's kindness was the first link in the chain of events that led to him coming to terms with his past. She'd seemed relieved and happy to hear Theron's thoughts. She had then wished him luck in the upcoming competition and told him to get a good night's rest. After hanging up the phone he had taken a shower and gone to bed.

Theron cracked open his eyelids and glanced back at the clock. There were still five minutes before the alarm would ring. He was starting to get bored of just lying around reminiscing, so he finally decided to get out of bed. He preemptively turned off the alarm and headed to the bathroom. Theron showered and got dressed in his gym clothes before he set out for the dining hall.

Theron started looking around for his classmates once he entered the dining hall. He spotted Vincent standing up and waving him over. Theron nodded back and pointed at the buffet, indicating he was going to grab breakfast before heading over to the table. After he got his food he walked over to where Vincent was seated. He saw Kaitlyn was also seated at the table, but none of their other classmates had arrived yet.

"Good morning," Theron greeted his two classmates as he sat down.

"Good morning," Vincent responded. Kaitlyn gave a little wave since she was still chewing on some food.

"So, what is the schedule for today?" Theron asked Vincent.

Vincent answered, "The competition will be starting at eight o'clock. Once everyone gets here I'll be announcing who will be participating in the first category of events. We'll try to stay together as much as we can throughout the day. If there is a need to do something outside the group, you should find someone else to go with you. Don't go anywhere on your own. It's not unheard of for some classes to use blackmail or detention strategies to cause disqualifications. You're new to the school, so I highly doubt you'll have to worry about being blackmailed, but some may try to capture you instead."

"That sounds pretty serious for just a school competition," Theron commented with concern.

Vincent shrugged with an amused grin. "Being able to deal with situations like that is also considered an important part of our education, so those kind of extreme strategies aren't discouraged. That being said, no one will try anything violent beyond simple restraints. Doing harm to another student is forbidden by the academy."

"I see," Theron answered. He continued to eat in silence, waiting for his other classmates to arrive. Alessia and Hikari came in together after a few minutes. They picked out what they wanted for breakfast and sat down at the table, quietly starting to eat. The same was repeated about a minute later when Nicholas, Darian, and Alonzo entered the dining hall together. Katerina came in next. She picked out her food and came to sit down next to Theron.

"Just waiting on the Frenchman," Nicholas observed with a bit of a sneer.

"If he's not here in five minutes we'll have to start the discussion without him," Vincent decided.

"Actually, I'm surprised Nicholas is here," Katerina commented. "I figured the members of the event committee would be gathering separately."

"I have to go in about fifteen minutes," Nicholas explained.

"I hope Jacques is okay," Hikari said in a worried tone.

"I'm sure he's just trying to be fashionably late," Alonzo tried to soothe Hikari's concern. "And if someone did do something to him, I'll make sure they regret it." Everyone in class usually picked on Jacques, but when all was said and done, the Frenchman was still a classmate, and his continued absence was starting to make everyone worried.

"I should have checked in on him at the dorm before I came over," Darian said with a frown.

"He's probably just getting as much sleep as he can. Despite his attitude, he's actually been pushing himself pretty hard in training. It's a little too soon to start worrying," Vincent said to calm everyone. Sure enough, within the next minute Jacques came walking into the dining hall.

"About time you got here," Nicholas scolded Jacques.

Jacques dismissed Nicholas's comment with a shrug. "There is still plenty of time until the competition. It hardly matters if I decided to sleep for a few extra minutes."

"Now that everyone is here, I'll go over our lineup

for the first category of events," Vincent announced. Everyone gave him their full attention. "The events of the first category will be held concurrently. Most of the students in the school have formal dance training, so the scores in that event will probably be fairly tight. Rather than contest such an even field, we'll participate in the more specialized figure skating and gymnastics events. Hikari and Alonzo will be participating in gymnastics. Alessia and I will compete in figure skating.

"I want everyone else to wait in the forested area south of the track. Stay out of the sunlight; it can drain your energy and make you sluggish. Also, stay away from crowds. Just try to relax in some place quiet and shady. Don't worry about cheering each other on at first; we'll save that for the endurance competition. Nicholas, since you're part of the committee, I'm going to give you our participation list for the day. Please handle all the entry procedures on our behalf."

Nicholas accepted an envelope from Vincent. "I'll take care of it. Since I'm not allowed to participate with you all, I'll do everything I can behind the scenes to help. Now I need to get going to the committee meeting. See you all later."

"All right everyone, this place is starting to fill up, so I think we're done for now. You all have free time till ten minutes before eight o'clock. Remember to move around in groups of two or more. We'll meet up in the athletics center before the opening announcements," Vincent instructed the group. Everyone acknowledged Vincent's instructions. Naturally, Katerina decided to pair up with Theron.

"So, what should we do until it's time to meet up with everyone?" Theron asked Katerina.

"How about we scout out the forest Vincent wanted us to stay in?" Katerina suggested. "We could try to look for a nice spot to relax."

"Sounds good to me," Theron agreed.

They wandered around the forest together. The entire forest was man-made, so the trees were intentionally arranged not to feel claustrophobic. However, the trees still created a canopy with only an occasional break to allow some sunlit clearings. The forest felt relaxing to Theron. It managed to avoid feeling gloomy, but also effectively blocked out direct sunlight. The trees themselves were only about fifteen meters tall, but they were still relatively young, and even though it didn't feel like it, they were above the tree line.

"Come to think of it, I wonder how they got these trees to grow at all at such a high elevation," Theron commented.

"Did you forget? I told you before they placed large heaters underground throughout campus," Katerina explained. "They warm up both the ground and the air above it enough to allow trees to grow normally. I believe I once heard that without the heaters, the air temperature here would be close to freezing during this time of year. As it is, if you were to climb up one of the trees you'd feel it growing much colder pretty quickly. The warmth starts to dissipate rapidly once you get about five meters off the ground. That's why none of the windows open above the first floor of any of the buildings."

It took Theron a moment to wrap his head around what Katerina told him. "I guess I didn't connect the heaters to the fact that trees grew normally. This place continues to amaze me. I wonder how the chairwoman manages to justify all the money and energy costs it must take to maintain this place. I mean, heating the entire campus from underground must be insanely expensive."

"I've heard several governments have given funding aid specifically for maintaining the higher temperature. Apparently they consider it an experiment worthy of long term research grants."

Theron shook his head at Katerina's explanation. "I guess I can see it happening if it's a case of government excess. I can't even imagine all the ways they could put that money to better use, but I guess I shouldn't complain given that I'm benefitting from that excess."

Katerina and Theron continued to chat until it was time to meet with their classmates again. They all gathered near the entrance of the athletics center and picked out seats in the indoor arena. As soon as it turned eight o'clock, the lights dimmed and a spotlight shown down on a podium placed on the arena floor. The Student Council President stepped into the light.

"Good morning everyone," Deacon greeted the student body. "I trust you're all ready to start the first competition of the school year. All of the event committee representatives should have reported the rules and order of events to their classes, so I only have one announcement to make before we get started. The class that wins the overall competition will be awarded with the right to advance their class rank by one level. So for example Class D could become Class C. If Class A wins, they can gain immunity from losing its level in a future event. Obviously this is a huge reward since higher ranked classes gain increased privileges over lower ranked classes. I hope that gets you all motivated to give it everything you've got today. I wish you all luck. Let the games begin!"

The student body let out a cheer to show their excitement. Committee members and adult staff members started placing dividers on the floor. Within about fifteen minutes the arena had been divided into three segments: a dance floor, a gymnastic area, and an ice rink. Apparently the facility had been built to be able to alter its floor type within minutes so it could host various events.

"Okay guys, all of you who aren't participating head on out," Vincent instructed. "In about forty-five minutes, start doing some warm up exercises. Don't push yourselves too hard. The track events will start at nine thirty. I'll see you all there.

Everyone nodded and then split up. The participants in the first category of events stayed behind, while the rest headed towards the forest. Once the group got to the area Katerina and Theron had picked out earlier, Theron laid down in a grassy spot and let his eyes drift shut. He let himself relax, but he kept his mind thinking about the events he was going to participate in keep from falling asleep.

After a few minutes, Theron began doing some psychic exercises the chairwoman had taught him shortly before the extended weekend. He began circulating the energy within his body. He hadn't had much time practicing these new skills, but the few times he had used them they had felt very natural. As he continued to circulate the energy, he slowly let it seep into his muscles. He could feel his body growing warmer. He continued the process, circulating his energy and infusing it into his physical body until it felt like the energy was moving on its own. He slowly allowed his concentration to fade, making sure the energy continued its motion even though he was using less of his focus to keep it going. Within about half an hour he could keep it circulating with no more than an occasional thought, prodding the energy along on its course.

"Theron, it's about time to start warming up," Katerina's voice called out to Theron. He opened his eyes and sat up. His body felt light. He pushed himself up off the ground with ease.

"Thanks Katerina," Theron said. "Guess I better start with a bit of light jogging, then stretching."

"Let's all jog together," Darian suggested as he came over.

Theron nodded and waited for everyone to gather before taking off at a relaxed jog. He didn't really feel like he needed to warm up, given how loose and warm his body already felt, but he decided it was best to keep up appearances. The hardest part about jogging in his present condition was maintaining his slow pace. His body, which was currently saturated with energy, screamed out that it wanted to go all out, but Theron held back.

After jogging for about five minutes in a wide circuit within the forest, Theron led everyone back to their starting point. Then everyone stretched for the remaining ten minutes before heading towards the track. Outside the stadium, they met up with Vincent and the others that had participated in the first few events.

"You all are looking well," Vincent commented on the group when they reunited. "We didn't do too badly at our events. We were eighth overall, but second among the second year high school students, so we've scored three points. Let's keep it up. For the track events, they're going to start with the shorter races and work their way up to the longer races. The track has nine lanes, but only the outside eight will be used in the sprinting events. Since they'll be able to run two full grade levels at the same time, they should advance through the competition fairly quickly. Theron, I want you to handle all the normal running events. Jacques, you'll be doing all the hurdle events. Relays will be held after the individual races. Darian will be the starter in all relays. The second runner will be Kaitlyn. The third runner will be Katerina, and the anchor will be

Theron."

"Theron impressed you that much?" Alessia asked in surprise. "You're going to run him ragged."

"Saying he impressed me is putting it lightly," Vincent responded. "He's going to shock everyone in the stadium. Theron, I want you to go all out at first, but if we have a strong lead, I want you to falter some in the longer distances. I want us to build up a big enough cushion in the early events that we can afford to lose a few later on. It'll allow us to give the impression that you're getting too tired to compete later. I'm hoping that will make everyone think we won't be using you after the track category, or at least that you don't have very good endurance. Of course, if we get close to dropping in the rankings you'll have to turn it back up, which would spoil the effect, so knowing when we're safe enough to start slacking off will be important. Those of us that participated in the first category will be taking our turn to rest in the forest. The envelope I gave Nicholas during breakfast contains all the registration information already, so you all won't need to worry about that. Kaitlyn, you'll be in charge of implementing the strategy and coming up with any additional tactics while I'm gone."

Kaitlyn nodded. "Leave it to me."

"All right, good luck everyone," Vincent said as he began to walk towards the forest. Hikari, Alonzo, and Alessia joined him.

"I guess Jacques and I will head over to the track since we're the only ones in the first few events." Theron lead everyone into the stadium

The five classmates split up when they got into the stadium. Jacques and Theron proceeded to the track while Katerina, Darian, and Kaitlyn headed up to the bleachers. A voice came over the stadium speaker system shortly after Theron and Jacques arrived on the field. "Congratulations to all those that did well in the first category of events. The track meet portion of today's schedule will begin momentarily. The two hurdle events will be first. Then the committee will clear off the track so we can begin the rest of the events."

"Sounds like our cue. Good luck Jacques." Theron clapped Jacques on the back.

"I do not need luck. Vincent seems to think you're some star athlete, but I'll show you that you are not a one man show," Jacques spat out the comment.

Theron was a bit taken aback, but given how prickly Jacques could be at times, he didn't really take the comment to heart. Instead he gave Jacques a firm nod. "Good. I don't intend to be a one man show, and if you can score us some early wins, it'll make our job that much easier later on. This is a team effort as far as I'm concerned."

Jacques gave Theron a snort, but didn't say anything further as he took his place in the lines of runners preparing to run the 110 meter hurdles. Theron waited on the field inside the track with the other runners waiting for their events. He made sure to pick out his classmates sitting on the bleachers and got their attention so they could keep an eye on him now that he was alone, then he focused on the starting area of the track. It looked like the junior high students were getting ready to begin their race. The first eight runners stood behind their blocks and waited for the starter.

After about a minute, a hush started to fall over the crowd as the starter raised his hands, signaling he was getting ready to begin the race. "Runners, on your marks." The runners got into their blocks and waited for the next command. "Set." The runners assumed their final starting positions, and within the next two seconds a shot rang out. The runners bolted out of their blocks.

Since these were middle school runners, Theron wasn't particularly interested in the results, but he paid close attention to how the runners pushed off the blocks. He didn't have much experience with blocks since he had usually started from a standing position in junior high, so he carefully observed the methods others used to get an idea of what to do when it was his turn to run.

The race was over in less than twenty seconds and four more runners stepped up to the blocks. These would be the third year junior high runners. Again Theron observed their starts carefully. These runners looked a little more refined and uniform in their starting methods. After the second heat was over, staff started to run out on the field and adjust the hurdle height to prepare for the high school heats.

Theron noticed Jacques approaching the blocks. It looked like the first and second year runners would be running together for the high school races as well. After about two minutes, the starter confirmed the hurdles had been adjusted and again signaled that he was ready to start the race. Theron tuned out all the noise and focused on the instant the race started. He adjusted the energy still circulating through him to increase his rate of perception, making his surroundings appear to slow down.

The moment the gun went off, only one runner was instantly out of the blocks, the other seven were a fraction of a second behind. Theron didn't recognize the runner that had managed such a perfect start, but the student was fast, too fast. Jacques was putting up a good fight, but he was falling behind the leader. By the end of the hundred ten meters Jacques was more than ten meters behind the leader, and the runner after him was about two strides further back. Theron looked at the time postings for the first time. The runner that won had posted a time that could make college level athletes jealous: just over thirteen seconds. Jacques came in second with a little under fifteen seconds.

When the placements were posted Theron realized the winner had been a first year, so Jacques had still placed first among the second years, but Theron knew better than to go over and congratulate him. Jacques was the kind of person who would just take offense since he had been beaten by a first year. He would probably feel like Theron was mocking him. The final heat started while Theron was thinking about the race. Most of the times from the third years were respectable, but none got even close to the first year.

After the final heat finished, staff members again ran out onto the field and began rearranging hurdles and adjusting their height. The junior high runners were instructed to take their place at the starting line for the two hundred meter distance, while high school runners were told to go to the four hundred meter starting line. The junior high event proceeded with very similar outcomes to the previous race in regards to which runners placed well. Most of the times were in the twenty-eight seconds range.

Within ten minutes, the rematch between the insanely fast first year and Jacques was about to begin in the 400 meter hurdles. Again, the first year got off to a perfect start, with practically no delay between the start signal and his push off the blocks. Everyone else had a longer delay. The results of the race were predictable enough based on the 110 meter hurdles. The first year crushed the other runners, posting a time under fifty seconds. The next closest was over fifty-four seconds. This time Jacques was third with just under fifty-five seconds.

Theron's classmate finished second among the second year students this time, but Class 2-B was still in the lead so far. Jacques jogged off the track after his race and collapsed on the field, covering his face with his hands. Theron motioned for his classmates to come down from the bleachers. Theron didn't pay attention to the final heat of the 400 meter hurdles. He waited for his classmates to cross over the track and join him. They all met around Jacques, but didn't try to offer words of sympathy. Instead, Theron suggested, "Why don't two of you take Jacques back to the forest since he's done with his event in this category. I'm sure you'll have time to come back before the relays start."

Kaitlyn nodded. "That sounds like a good idea. Katerina and Darian can take Jacques back. I'll stay here with Theron in case I need to make a strategic change. I wasn't expecting a runner like that from the first years. Hopefully he'll be tired out and won't be in any more events for a while."

Katerina seemed to hesitate, but ultimately she and Darian agreed and helped Jacques off the ground. Jacques gave Theron a blank stare before walking off with his two escorts. The staff members had just about finished removing the hurdles from the track. "I'm going to get ready for the next race," Theron declared and started walking towards the starting line for the 100 meter dash.

Once he got to the area where the runners were gathering, Theron immediately noticed the first year that had beat Jacques. The boy wasn't breathing hard, but his eyes were bloodshot. Theron watched the first year carefully. He realized something wasn't normal about the boy, but he couldn't quite figure out what. The sound of the starter pistol signaling the start of the first junior high heat drew Theron's attention back to the other runners. With probably only a minute to go before his heat started, Theron started circulating his energy faster, trying to strengthen his body to its limits.

He strained his perception so much that by the time the shot rang out starting the second junior high heat it seemed like nearly a second passed before the runners crawled out of their blocks.

Finally it was time for Theron's heat. He slowly approached the blocks. At least, he thought he was moving slowly, but he noticed that the other runners were moving as if walking against a strong current. Theron had to consciously slow himself down even more so he didn't appear too abnormal. He got down in the blocks and made adjustments to them so they felt comfortable, but would still give him a compact position to explode out from. After finishing his adjustments, Theron stood by the blocks.

He waited for what seemed like minutes before the starter signaled that he was ready to start the race. Theron could barely make out what the starter was saying because his words had become so drawn out, but Theron knew based on the procedures what he had to do. He made sure to wait until the starter finished speaking before he repositioned himself in the blocks. There was a long pause before the command to get set came. Theron raised his bottom and looked out straight ahead of him, his hands positioned just behind the starting line and holding a good portion of his body weight. He waited to hear the low pitch of the starting signal. He shifted his eyes to see when the smoke would start to come out of the starter pistol.

Finally it came, and he leaped forward. He kept his body low for the first several paces, slowly rising up to his full height as he ran. He didn't even try to look at the other runners. He allowed his vision to form a tunnel. The only things Theron saw were the lane stretching out in front of him and the finish line. He drove his legs as hard as he could. Thanks to reinforcing his phsyical strength with his life energy, each stride carried him well over two meters. His enhanced perception allowed him to feel the instant each foot began to come into contact with the ground, allowing him to dig his toes into the track and push himself into his next stride before the impact could cause him to lose any forward momentum. It took Theron less than ten seconds to break through the tape at the finish line.

As soon as he finished the race Theron turned and noticed the first year less than half a second behind him, crossing over before the tape had time to fall. The boy looked at Theron with a dumbfounded expression, completely surprised that someone had beaten him. Theron's suspicions grew deeper. Theron hadn't held back his speed, and with him reinforcing his body there should have been no way any normal person could have kept up with him, especially not someone near his own age. Maybe the boy was using some performance enhancing drugs. That might also explain his bloodshot eyes. But why would a student do that just to do well in a school athletic competition? Was it even possible for a drug to increase performance so much that a high school student could compete on a world stage?

Theron shook the questions from his mind. Answering those questions didn't matter. All that mattered was making sure his team did well enough to win the day. When Theron broke his attention away from the first year, he noticed the stadium was almost silent. All the cheering had ceased, and was replaced by a kind of shocked awe. He saw Kaitlyn coming towards him, her eyes were wide open, and she seemed almost dazed. Theron walked over to meet her.

"What's wrong? Why is everyone so quiet?" Theron asked Kaitlyn.

Kaitlyn worked her mouth silently as she pointed at the time postings. Finally some words came out. "You just broke the world record by almost a tenth of a second. How is that even possible?"

Theron blinked a few times, not really comprehending what he had done. When it finally settled in he cursed himself. He hadn't meant to break any records. He just wanted to be sure that he beat that first year. He realized he should have held back a little more, but wasn't sure how to balance staying ahead but still holding back against an opponent like that. The first year had managed to post a time just under ten seconds as well. There was only one thing he could really think of to say to Kaitlyn. "I didn't mean to. I just wanted to win."

Kaitlyn's expression of shock grew more pronounced. "Is this what Vincent saw in you? That's why he put you in every running event?"

"Well, I didn't push quite as hard when Vincent was testing me," Theron admitted.

Kaitlyn just shook her head. "Well, I guess at this point we don't really need to change our strategy. Vincent had said you would shock everyone in the stadium, so I guess this is still within his plans. Still, I didn't think even he expected this much. I understand it's hard to hold back in the sprint distances, but as the races get longer you may want to slow it down a little. Obviously you should still try to place first among the second years, but you don't really need to go smashing every record there is."

"Yeah, I'm sorry about that," Theron apologized.

Kaitlyn just shook her head again. "You should head over to the starting line for the two hundred meter distance. It looks like the crowd is starting to recover, so the last heat for the hundred should start soon."

"All right," Theron agreed. He started heading over to the starting line for his next event. It only took about five minutes for his turn to come. The audience seemed to hush in anticipation this time, wanting to see the next race between the two runners that could move faster than any high school student should be able to. Theron continued to keep his perception rate high so he could have a perfect start, and he continued to reinforce his strength to keep his stride length long, but he allowed his feet to make more contact with the ground, slowing himself a fraction with each step. He started to fine tune his running so he wouldn't create a big scene like he had before. This time he managed to stay away from the world record, but he still ran two hundred meters in just under twenty seconds. This time the first year almost caught him, but Theron wasn't as concerned by it this time.

Kaitlyn nodded at him after he finished, giving her approval to his slow down. Theron noticed the first year had also started glaring at him, but Theron just shrugged it off. He just waited for his next race which would start in about ten minutes. While he was waiting, Katerina and Darian returned.

The first words out of their mouths when they met Theron were predictable. "We heard rumors on the way here that you broke a world record earlier."

Theron felt a little sheepish. "Yeah, I didn't really mean to, but you remember how fast that first year was. I just wanted to make sure I beat him."

Darian blinked a few times. "Wow, I wish I could break a record just because I wanted to beat someone. What are you? You're a genius in both athletics and academics? You're abilities are beyond being abnormal. They're even beyond incredible. You're unique, and don't get me wrong, I'm glad you're on my team, but frankly your abilities are little scary."

"Well, I don't think he's scary," Katerina commented. "I couldn't be prouder of having a brother like Theron."

"Brother?" Darian questioned the two while Kaitlyn quirked an eyebrow at Katerina's declaration.

"Yeah, I guess Katerina's the only one in our class that knows the details from my past," Theron explained. "To make a long story short, I was orphaned when I was ten years old and sent to an orphanage by a corrupt executor of my parents' will. My parents had actually meant for me to be adopted by Katerina's parents. It was a happy twist of fate that brought Katerina and I together on this campus. Over this past weekend I got to meet Katerina's parents and they arranged to officially adopt me. So Katerina and I are now siblings. Anyway, I better get ready for my next event." Theron rushed through the explanation and turned to walk back towards the track. He didn't really want to go in to the details of what had happened, so he hadn't given the others chance to question him further. He could faintly hear Katerina being interrogated instead as he continued to walk away. His next race would be starting in less than three minutes.

Theron waited patiently until it was his turn. He ran four hundred meters in the same manner he had run two hundred meters. He intentionally adjusted the amount of impact he let his body absorb before beginning his next stride so he could maintain precise control over his speed. He still posted times that would win him any track meet on the collegiate level, and he still edged out the first year, but he stayed far away from any extreme times.

After his third race Kaitlyn advised him to slow down even more. It was time for him to start giving the impression that he was getting tired, or was poor at longer distances. Theron's time in the 100-meter dash and his relatively slower times in the races since would also feed in to that perception. During the eight hundred meter distance Theron allowed the first year to pass him for the first time. After the race, the first year had sneered at Theron triumphantly, not understanding that Theron had let him win.

During the 1500-meter run Theron slowed down even more, allowing his full foot to come in contact with the track. He slowed down so much that his first year competitor ended up beating him by over almost a hundred meters. He even allowed another runner to pass him, making him the second place finisher amongst the second year students. After the race he made a show of resting his hands on his knees and hanging his head down.

Theron's teammates helped sell the act by showing concern for him, though their eyes were all smiling. The individual events were over, and it was time for the relays to begin. Kaitlyn started adding up points accumulated so far and comparing them to the possible points remaining. "Okay everyone. With the current point spread, we only need to place second in one of the four relays. We can be third in the other three. Given that there will be no real breaks between events, we'll have to make the second place finish our first race so we can continue the appearance of Theron being too tired to compete effectively. We need to all run as fast as we can so Theron can run poorly but still get second."

Katerina and Darian nodded at Kaitlyn's instructions. The four headed to their positions for the 4 x 100 meter relay. They had to wait another ten minutes for the race to start. Theron decided not to increase his perception rate for this race, and he even weakened the reinforcement to his body. He didn't feel physically sore or tired, but he did feel drained by all the energy he had spent so far. It wouldn't affect his performance much though. Even before he had learned to use his life energy to infuse his physical body he had been a fast runner. Theron focused his attention on the starting group.

Finally Theron could see smoke rising from the starter pistol and he heard the shot a moment later. Darian got off to a good start and was running hard. He was in second place when he handed his baton to Kaitlyn.

Kaitlyn was a rather tall American. She was surprisingly athletic for how quiet she usually was, and she did an impressive job, but she was slowly being overtaken by another runner. She had dropped down to third place by the time she handed the baton to Katerina.

Katerina appeared to have no athletic ability to speak of. She tried her best, and luckily she had enough of a lead that a couple of the runners couldn't pass her, but she still fell to sixth place when she handed off the Baton to Theron. He took off running. He felt so slow and heavy compared to how he had felt in his earlier races. The formerly well-defined impact of his feet hitting the track felt dull, but he charged forward as hard as he could, trying to make up lost ground. He managed to overtake two runners, but he ran out of track before he could advance back into third place. He hung his head at the fourth place finish.

"What are you so upset about?" Darian asked as he came over to the finish line.

"We didn't get second," Theron stated dejectedly.

"That's true. We actually got first among the second years. I guess we should have hung back just a bit more, but it's hard to figure out exactly where you need to place in these circumstances." Darian shrugged.

"First? What do you mean?" Theron asked.

Darian smiled at Theron. "Don't you remember? Girls' times are normalized, and the only teams that beat us were all-boys teams. I figure we'll jump ahead of the other second year teams by a second or so. Just wait till they finish calculating the places, then you'll see."

Sure enough, within a minute, the results were posted. Theron's class had managed to take first place in the second year high school group after the times of the girls were adjusted. "I guess that means we can get by without even placing in an event then," Theron commented.

"It's better than that," Kaitlyn said as she joined Darian and Theron. "The second place overall in our grade didn't get second in this event, so we have even more breathing room. We can actually lose every event now and still win first overall, so let's just run for fun now. Theron also did a great job, even though he still ran pretty fast, it was nothing like the times he was getting in the sprints at the beginning of the meet, so let's just keep it up. Let's get ready for the next race."

The team broke up again to take their assigned positions for the next relay. It started within a couple of minutes. They still seemed like they were running pretty hard, but running fast without any pressure felt completely different from running fast because a person had to. Theron, however, still had a problem. He had to keep adjusting his pace to show that he was getting slower, but not drop off so much in any one race that it would make people suspicious that he was slowing down intentionally. As a result, even though they didn't need to win, Theron's team still placed second in their grade.

The next relay required each member to run four hundred meters. Theron's team took a more relaxed pace this time, but still tried to put some pressure on the other runners, making it look like they were trying to keep up, and then letting Theron fall behind. They didn't place at all in the third relay.

Before the sprint medley relay could start, Theron brought the team together to make a suggestion. "I think we should withdraw from the final race. It's clear by the point totals that we've won already anyway, and I think it would show how tired I am more effectively if we forfeit completely."

Kaitlyn nodded at the proposal. "That sounds like a good plan, especially since we didn't place for the first time in that last event. Let's all go up to the registration desk and let them know. We should all visually support Theron, making a show of him being too tired to run when he doesn't need to."

The four headed over to the registration desk and declared their intent to forfeit the final race due to the exhaustion of a team member. The committee members immediately nodded their heads and commented on what a tremendous effort Theron had put forth. Theron thanked them for their kind words before heading back to the forest to meet up with the rest of the class.

Vincent greeted them as they arrived. "Welcome back. Did the plan work out?"

Kaitlyn answered. "We won the category by enough of a margin to forfeit the last event under the pretext that Theron was too tired to continue. By the way, next time you should tell me when you find a monster athlete. Watching this guy race for the first time was bad for my heart."

Vincent smiled. "Fast isn't he?"

Kaitlyn gave Vincent a flat look. "He broke the world record in the 100 meter dash."

Vincent's eyes widened a bit at Kaitlyn's statement. "I admit I wasn't expecting that. Still, that makes me more confident in my decision for the third category. Theron, I want you to compete in the one hour decathlon. I hope your stamina can hold up, but if you can make it through this you'll be able to rest during the entire swimming competition. Alessia, as our best all-around athlete I want you to take on the triathlon. I'll race in the marathon. Let's all head back to the stadium."

Jacques approached Theron as the class headed out of the forest. "So you managed to win most of your events after all." Jacques tone seemed subdued, but his eyes almost seemed to burn with envy, maybe even hate.

"It would have been much harder without the points you earned us at the beginning," Theron pointed out in hopes of soothing Jacques ego. "Anyway, we should get going." Theron followed after his other classmates. He could hear Jacques trudging behind him.

Once they got back to the stadium, Vincent gave more instructions. "All right, Theron, you head into the track stadium. Alessia, the triathlon is starting at the outdoor pool, so you head over there. Everyone else is free to split up to cheer for whomever they wish, but remember to stay in groups."

Everyone acknowledged Vincent's instructions as they began to split up. Theron headed back into the stadium. Because the one hour decathlon was the least time consuming of the three endurance events, it had a much larger opening window for a start time. The endurance competition was allowed to run for up to three hours, so as long as an athlete started the one hour decathlon within ninety minutes of that deadline he or she would be able to comfortably finish in time. Since most teams didn't have the luxury of leaving all the track events from the previous category on one or two people, many athletes were taking advantage of the format to take a break and rest before beginning. Theron knew that could create a bottleneck as everyone would have to wait on one another to start their events, so he decided to start as soon as he could.

Theron walked up to the registration table and told the students there that he wanted to start his decathlon immediately. The committee members, which were different than the ones at the table when he had declared he would forfeit the last relay, looked at Theron as if dumbstruck. Theron guessed anyone would be surprised to see him start the decathlon so soon after the track meet. He realized that reaction had been part of what Vincent had planned. Even after his showing in the beginning of the track meet, by slowing down as the meet went on Theron had successfully managed everyone's expectations to believe he wouldn't be as big of a threat in the endurance category. They were probably surprised he was participating at all. Everyone just stared at Theron as he approached the starting line for the hundred meter portion of the decathlon.

Theron didn't try to go all out like he had in the first event of the track meet, but he still increased the amount of energy he was using to strengthen his body. It almost felt like he was taking a stroll when he posted a time just over ten seconds. Theron moved on to the long jump. His enhanced leg strength allowed him to jump just short of eight meters. As Theron jogged over to the shot put circle he noticed several athletes starting up their decathlons. He was almost surprised he didn't see the first year that had competed with him in the track meet.

Theron flew through the events. There were no other participants ahead of him, so he didn't have to wait between events. He racked up over forty-six hundred points in the first five events, but he dropped off pace during the sixth event. He had never jumped hurdles before, so he didn't have a good technique. The hurdles slowed him down significantly more than they should have, and he barely managed to break sixteen seconds, gaining less than eight hundred points. His discuss throw went well, but he had trouble with the pole vault technique, barely clearing four meters. The javelin throw was also deceptively more difficult than Theron thought it would be. He was able to build up plenty of speed, but transitioning from the run to the throw proved difficult. Ultimately Theron only threw about sixty meters.

Theron reached the final event, the 1,500 meter run, within forty minutes of starting his decathlon. He started running at a good pace, but after the first eight hundred meters Theron began to falter. At first he didn't know what was happening. His legs suddenly started feeling like lead, and he felt exhausted. It took him a few moments to realize his life energy was running dangerously low. He wasn't able to keep the energy circulating properly, so his reinforcement had stopped. Apparently the energy didn't prevent his body from getting tired; it only masked the feeling. With his support gone, Theron felt his fatigue hit him hard. He almost stumbled on the track, but managed to catch himself. He couldn't remember ever feeling so weak. He forced himself to continue, but his pace had slowed to a crawl. He had completed the first eight hundred meters in less than two minutes, but it took him over three minutes to complete the remaining seven hundred meters.

After he had finished the race Theron trudged off the track and collapsed on the field. He didn't think he'd be able to move for a while. To make matters worse, he didn't have the concentration to drain energy from specific people around him any longer. He could only pull energy in indiscriminately. Soon he had to keep himself from even doing that much as Katerina rushed onto the field to check on him.

"Theron, are you okay?" Katerina asked with a tone

that let Theron know how intensely worried she was.

Theron commanded his body to sit up. It was an enormous struggle, but he managed it. "I'll be fine, I'm just worn out. I gave it everything I had."

Jacques and Alonzo came towards Theron. Apparently they had also decided to cheer him on. Theron was surprised to see Jacques, but Alonzo explained, "We figured you'd be done with your event first, so we decided to watch you crush your opponents before heading over to watch the other two. You did an amazing job. You could easily compete on the world stage if you wanted to, and you're just a high school student. It makes me want to work even harder. I'm really touched by your competitive spirit."

"That's enough Alonzo," Jacques said as he reached out his hand towards Theron. "The man is obviously exhausted. I'll take him back to the forest. You two can go cheer on our classmates."

Katerina hesitated, but Alonzo agreed and started dragging her off. "We'll be heading off to the triathlon." Theron nodded in response to Alonzo's declaration and took Jacques hand. He managed to pull himself to his feet. His body was feeling sorer as time went on. He tried to manipulate his energy to help with the soreness, but it wasn't responding. Jacques slowed his pace to match Theron's pained motions as the two left the stadium.

"You really look like you need a break. Come over here," Jacques suggested. "I must admit, I never thought you would really be so talented as an athlete, but I also never thought you'd burn yourself out so much. You really aren't as smart as you seem."

"You may be right," Theron agreed with a bit of self-derision. He really didn't need to try so hard. He could have paced himself better. Still, he was surprised by the tone Jacques had used to give his critique.

Theron had never been on good terms with Jacques, and things had seemed to be taking a turn for the worse today, but maybe Jacques was also a little touched by Theron's effort.

The thought was short lived though. Once they reached a more isolated spot that Jacques was leading them towards, several students approached him. When the students came close, Jacques shoved Theron to the ground and sneered, "You really are stupid. You guys can take care of this idiot. I'm going to go back to my classmates and try to divert their suspicions for a while."

Theron looked at Jacques in shock. Sure, he knew his classmate hated him, but Theron had no idea Jacques would go this far. "Why are you doing this?"

"Because it's in my best interest, of course," Jacques answered as if it were the most obvious thing in the world before he walked away.

The other students advanced towards Theron. He guessed they were also second years, but he didn't recognize any of them. "Now you don't need to worry mister scholarship student," one of the students said. "We'll follow the rules not to inflict any harm on you. But we're going to have to take you out of the competition. I imagine your team will let you rest up during the swimming category, letting you crush everyone in the final event, but we can't let that happen."

Theron couldn't help smiling. He remembered another lesson the chairwoman had taught him shortly after he had started feeding on other students' life energy. At the time, the lesson had been meant to help him know when to stop draining energy before it started producing noticeable effects. Now he spun that lesson on its head. He no longer tried to hold back his body's instinct to draw energy from its surroundings.

He pulled hard on the life energy within the students around him. Rather than slowly draining energy, suddenly pulling out large amounts of energy could render his victims unconscious. If he pulled out more he could even threaten their lives, but he didn't want to go that far. The students around him suddenly started to look dazed. Some of them even stumbled.

Draining energy this fast in an area attack wasn't a very efficient way to restore energy, but because of the quantity being taken it still did a good job. Theron's fatigue faded and he stood up. His body felt light again, but he couldn't stop there. Now that he had recovered enough to fully control his energy again, he started making specific psychic attacks, draining energy even faster from his would-be assailants. It was only a few moments before they collapsed, twitching on the ground.

When Theron confirmed that they were incapacitated, though not permanently harmed, he tried reproducing the attack Trish had performed on him on his first night on campus. He sent energy directly into the students' minds, focusing on the region of the brain responsible for short term memory. He sent a small burst of energy to disrupt any memories from forming, ensuring that the students wouldn't remember this encounter. In fact, they probably wouldn't remember anything from the entire day. Once Theron was done, he jogged away from the unconscious students. He proceeded to one of the medical stations set up for the day and informed a nurse that he had discovered some unconscious students. She contacted the medical facility and requested that staff come to the location. The students were removed from the scene within about five minutes.

"It appears they are stable, and able to respond to stimuli. It doesn't appear to be anything too serious, but we'll keep them under observation for a little while to be safe. I'll interview them after they wake up so we can learn what might have happened. Thank you for bringing this to our attention." The nurse thanked Theron.

"I was just doing my duty as a health officer." Theron answered as he walked away from the medical station. Next he decided to find Jacques and give the traitor a good scare. He headed towards the outdoor bleachers set up to watch the triathlon. He spotted his classmates easily enough and walked over to them.

Katerina saw Theron first. "Theron! Are you feeling better already? Jacques said you told him you wanted to rest in the forest alone until the final event."

Theron watched Jacques expression with satisfaction as the traitor turned to face him. Theron turned back to Katerina. "Oh, I'll go back to resting soon, I just wanted to let you know I was feeling much better. Jacques gave me a great energy boost."

"Oh, that's out of character for him," Katerina said thoughtfully.

Jacques had turned as pale as a sheet. "That is very rude. I am capable of being thoughtful." Even though the words Jacques used were normal, his delivery didn't have any of its usual bite.

Alonzo clapped Jacques on the back. "Are you okay? You aren't looking too well."

Jacques looked around before answering, "I think there may be too many people here. I'm starting to feel a little sick. I think I'll go take a rest in my room. Vincent didn't have anything else planned for me today anyway."

Alonzo nodded. "Take care of yourself."

Jacques nodded weakly and made his escape. Theron smiled to himself. Now he had an advantage he could hold over Jacques. Theron didn't plan to expose the Frenchman, but he would use what had happened to make Jacques feel indebted to him. With luck, maybe Theron could convince Jacques he wasn't an enemy. A lot of luck. At very least, Theron could ensure Jacques caused no problems in the future. Theron turned his attention back to his other classmates. "Well, I'm going to go eat lunch and then take a nap at our spot in the forest. You can have someone wake me up when it's time for the final event."

"I'll go with you," Katerina volunteered. "Alonzo, you can tell the others to meet there after these races are finished, right?"

"Sure." Alonzo nodded.

Theron and Katerina started walking towards the dining hall together. Katerina talked about how amazing he was as an athlete while Theron, feeling embarrassed, demurred in the face of all the compliments. After all, it wasn't like he was really competing fairly. He really didn't feel like he deserved any praise, but he also didn't want to put a damper on Katerina's enthusiasm, so he didn't really try to stop her from complimenting him either. The two ate lunch at a leisurely pace since they had about two hours before the next category of competitions would begin.

After they had finished eating they returned to the forest. As they were getting settled in, Katerina tapped Theron on the shoulder and looked up into his eyes. "If you're going to sleep, why don't you lay your head down on my lap?"

Theron smiled at the offer. "Sure you won't get tired? I might be resting for a while."

"That's fine," Katerina answered with a smile. "If my legs start going numb I'll just toss you off."

"You're so generous," Theron commented sarcastically, but he laid his head on Katerina's lap and closed his eyes. After a few minutes he could hear

Katerina begin to hum softly, but he didn't recognize the tune. It was soothing enough to help him drift to sleep though.

He vaguely felt his head being lifted up and set gently on the ground at some point, but it wasn't enough to really wake him up. Eventually Theron opened his eyes. It was getting dark, which meant he had probably slept for almost five hours. He looked around and spotted Vincent and Alessia sitting near him.

"I see you're finally awake," Vincent commented when he saw Theron looking at him. "The others went to the swimming competition a few hours ago. They should be done before too long. I understand you did really well in the decathlon. Alessia and I did alright, and when our results were combined with your score we managed to get first in the endurance category among the second year high school classes, but man, I have to tell you there is a monster first year competing. He ran the marathon in about two hours and ten minutes. The next place was almost twenty minutes behind him."

"I think I know who you're talking about," Theron said. "It's probably the same first year that Jacques and I ran against in the track events."

"So that's the kid the others were talking about when they brought Jacques back after his hurdling events?" Vincent shook his head in amazement. "I thought having one monster athlete was enough, but I guess we have two at this academy. I'm just glad he's not in our year. As long as you can pull through in the last event, we should win the overall competition. We'll probably even end up with the highest score out of all the grades. Are you feeling up to it?"

"I'm well rested now. It shouldn't be a problem," Theron answered.

"All right, then lets head to the swimming pool. No sense in making the others walk all the way here just to have them walk all the way back," Vincent said as he got up. Alessia and Theron also stood up and the three started walking out of the forest. They arrived at the pool just in time to see the last event in the swimming category: the 4x200 meter freestyle relay. Theron noticed Katerina was part of the team.

"Is Katerina a good swimmer?" Theron asked Vincent. "I watched her during the track relays and she doesn't strike me as a good athlete."

Vincent gave Theron a dubious look. "You two spend all that time together and you don't know? She's a poor runner, but if you put that girl in the water she's practically a fish. She's without a doubt the best swimmer in our class. Even if you don't normalize her times, she'll beat any of us boys."

Theron was surprised to hear Vincent's analysis, but he turned his attention back towards the pool to watch. Apparently Katerina was going to be the anchor. Hikari was the first swimmer. It was only about two minutes until the race was about to start.

Hikari got up on her starting block and waited. When the event finally began she dove into the water. Theron didn't know much about swimming, so he couldn't analyze strokes or anything, but he could tell that Hikari was doing well, given that she was keeping up with the lead swimmers. After she swam four lengths of the pool, the second swimmer for the team, Alonzo, dived into the pool. Alonzo started off in fourth, but was within a meter of the leader. He slowly started gaining on them, managing to get into the lead by hand length by the time Darian jumped into the pool. Darian wasn't as strong a swimmer as Alonzo was, and it didn't take long for other swimmers to start catching him. He barely managed to stay within two meters of the leader by the end of his two hundred meters. He was in fifth place.

When Katerina dove into the water and started swimming, Theron couldn't help but be a little mesmerized. She didn't look like she was swimming as much as she was gliding across the surface of the waters. The water carried Katerina forward. Within the first hundred meters she had managed to work her way up to second. When they got to the end of the race Katerina was almost half a body length ahead.

"Unfortunately it's not enough," Vincent commented as he looked at the overall results for the swimming competition. "Given that Katerina was still able to put forth such a strong performance, maybe I should have entrusted more events to her. Oh well, third place in the category is fine. Now it's all in your hands Theron."

"All right, I'm just going to let Katerina know she did a good job before I head over to the stadium," Theron said as he got out of his seat.

He went down to where Katerina was standing and gave her a quick hug. When he saw her looking shocked he decided to explain himself. "My way of congratulating you. You did a really great job. I only got to see the last event, but you were amazing."

Katerina blushed at Theron's compliments. "Thank you."

"I'm going to go over to the track stadium and get ready for the last event," Theron said as he started to walk away. For some reason seeing Katerina embarrassed was making him feel embarrassed too. He entered the stadium that was only about twenty-five meters from the pool. When he got inside he saw that the obstacle course had been set up in the center of the field. It actually looked like a fairly simple course with only four stages. A table was placed before each stage.

Theron assumed the tables were for taking the academic tests.

The first stage was a ten meter high rock wall that had to be climbed. The second obstacle was a five meter long balance beam that looked only about five centimeters wide. The third stage had a series of ropes hanging down from a beam. They got longer the further away from the platform they got. Under all but the last few ropes there was a water pit, so Theron guessed the goal was for the participants to swing themselves from rope to rope until they eventually got to the ropes that dropped all the way to the dry ground. The fourth stage seemed to require the competitors to crawl through a maze of tunnels only about a meter tall. That structure looked like it'd be the biggest challenge due more to the maze configuration than the actual crawling.

Overall the obstacles weren't too bad, which probably meant the academic questions would be pretty nasty. Theron walked to the starting line and waited for the other competitors to arrive. It didn't take very long. The students were rushed into the stadium by the event committee members and staff so the competition could come to a close before it got too dark.

Proctors took their places in front of each of the obstacles. The proctor for the first stage explained the rules to the participants. "Once I have given you all permission to begin, each of you will pick a seat at the table. Tests have already been placed face down at each seat. All the tests are the same, so it doesn't matter where you sit. When you start the test, identify which class you are part of on the paper. I will ensure that no one cheats off another participant's test. Once you have completed your test you may attempt the obstacle. When you arrive at the next proctor you must take another test them before moving on. If you fail any obstacle you must return to the beginning of that obstacle until it is completed successfully. You will not be asked to take the same test twice. Are there any questions?" No one spoke. "Very well, you may begin."

Everyone rushed over to the tables and claimed a seat. Theron sat down and flipped his paper over, revealing the questions. It looked like the subject for the first test was math. There was a mix of algebra, calculus, and trigonometry questions. There was no requirement to show any work, so Theron only had to write the answers. He flew through the questions with ease. Within five minutes, he had managed to finish the test. Theron made sure to identify his class on the paper and turned the test in to the proctor. The proctor glanced at the test and waved Theron on.

Theron quickly climbed up the rock wall. It wasn't very difficult, and it made Theron wondered if they had scaled back the physical difficulty to accommodate people who spent most of their time studying and hadn't spent time developing their physical capabilities. It didn't really matter though. It was probably obvious to everyone at the beginning that this event was more focused on academics.

Theron reached the next station. He was surprised to see that some other students had already started climbing the rock wall behind him. He thought the first test would have slowed them down a bit more. Theron sat at the second table and flipped over his test. It was a science test covering chemistry, physics, and biology. This test took Theron longer to complete. The section that required labeling every bone in the human body was particularly time consuming as Theron tried to recall books he had read years ago. One of the other students managed to overtake Theron while he was working, putting him in second place.

Theron turned in his test and started chasing after

the other student as soon as the proctor waved him on. There were several balance beams to choose from so that multiple students could cross at one time. Theron practically ran across one of the beams, regaining the lead over the other student who was shuffling his feet to maintain full contact with the beam at all times.

Theron sat at the table before the third obstacle. This test was several pages long. When Theron flipped it over, he realized it was a reading comprehension test. It might be a nasty test if the reader didn't know English very well, but Theron guessed all the students that attended the academy would be fairly proficient, so it wouldn't really be a hard test for anyone, more of a speed reading test really. Theron had spent most of his spare time at the orphanage reading, and he had gotten very good at reading quickly. He read three pages in about a minute and began answering questions about the material. He was finished in short order.

Theron handed in the reading test and grabbed hold of the first rope in the next obstacle. He swung to the next rope and grabbed it. He let the first rope pull him back some before releasing it and swinging forward on the second rope. As he swung he let himself slide down the rope a little. He grabbed the third rope and repeated the process. The ropes were getting further apart as they got longer, but Theron kept his swinging momentum going, so he was able to cross at a rapid pace.

When he reached the fourth table the proctor stopped him and carefully inspected Theron, probably ensuring that he hadn't landed in the water and decided to skip ahead. The proctor gave Theron a nod and allowed him to take the next test. This test was ten pages long and filled with logic problems. Theron couldn't help but think this entire event had been made for him. He had always loved logic puzzles. Some of the questions were pretty tricky. They were written to make a person think in a specific way, but often the solution required a person to mentally step back and rethink through the problem in different ways. It was fun for Theron, but while he was reasoning out the problems more students started to catch up. Theron wasn't too concerned though. He had started the test first, and he was convinced he would finish it first. He didn't let his surroundings distract or rush him as he worked his way through the test, considering each problem carefully.

When Theron finished the test and looked up, he noticed that three other students had turned in the test before him. That shook Theron a little bit. He rushed over to the proctor with his test. As soon as the proctor gave him permission, Theron practically dove into the tunnel maze. It didn't take Theron long to realize the tunnel had some nasty tricks. In places, the tunnels had been divided in half, forcing a leopard crawl instead of a standard crawl. To make matters worse, one couldn't be sure if the top half and bottom half followed the same path. The maze hadn't looked too bad from the outside, but once Theron got inside he found out that what had appeared to be four-way connections had paths internally walled off, further complicating the maze. Luckily, Theron could see pretty well even in this darkness, so at least he wouldn't go all the way down a dead end.

Theron also had one other advantage he could use. He started relying on his mind's eye to see the traces of energy people had left behind. He could see where the people that had entered before him had gone. Theron could tell when someone had doubled back, and he could also see their present locations. The physical barriers in the way didn't matter. So far, no one had begun exploring the upper half of the paths. So Theron climbed up the nearest junction he could find. Since he also left an energy trail, he never had to worry about accidently exploring the same section twice. As Theron progressed through the maze, he started building a map inside his head. He used the upper path to crawl over a couple of the other students that had entered before him. Theron was starting to feel more confident that he was in the lead.

Eventually Theron had mapped out enough of the maze to start figuring out the patterns. More students were making it into the maze, but no one had found the exit yet. A few had started exploring the upper tunnels though. Theron started to move with more confidence as he gained more information about the mazes layout. He started to pick out a route to the end rather than just exploring the maze. Within the following three minutes he had managed to find the way out. He had spent a total of twenty-two minutes in the maze. His total course time was sixty-three minutes, and he answered all his test questions correctly, so he suffered no penalties. Theron had managed to seal up Class 2-B's victory in the overall competition.

Theron's classmates came to meet him after his results were posted. They all cheered for him, and Katerina returned his hug from earlier. Jacques was still absent, but that was expected. Everyone waited for the other competitors to finish up the obstacle course. It took about another forty minutes for the first place finishers from all the other grades to be determined. Since it was a winner-take-all format, the committee began leading all the other contestants out of the maze once the first place winners were established.

A few minutes after the last event officially ended. The Student Council President's voice came over the stadium speaker system. "Congratulations to all of you for making it through the first competition of the school year. I know you all are probably ready to get out of here, so I just wanted to make a quick announcement. The awards and rewards for this competition will be handed out this Friday in an afternoon assembly. Any class rank changes will take effect next week. With that announcement, I declare this athletic competition officially over. Have a good night."

Vincent clapped his hands to get everyone's attention. "Well, I want to thank you all for following my lead today. For my final instruction for the day, I say we all get something to eat before splitting up. I guess it wouldn't be right to start up the main celebrations until Jacques is here too, but surely a little party during dinner would be all right. Tomorrow during class we'll have the real celebration, and we can all talk about what we'll do next week when we become the new Class A."

Everyone agreed. Theron and his classmates headed over to the dining hall, exchanging stories about the events they participated in during the day. Theron described the tests and the tunnel from the final event, but he didn't go into too much detail on his other events, relying on his classmates that witnessed them to tell the stories. The class stayed in the dining hall until it was almost nine o'clock at night. As they were splitting up, the nurse that Theron had talked to earlier about the students he had left unconscious saw him and came over to talk. Theron waved his classmates on ahead, wishing them a good night.

"I just wanted to let you know that those boys all woke up and don't appear to be suffering any physical harm, but none of them can remember what they were doing there, or anything else about today," the nurse told Theron.

"Well, the important thing is they're okay." Theron hid his relief that he had succeeded in wiping out their memories. "Maybe after a few days they'll remember what happened and explain it to you."

"I hope so," the nurse responded. "Anyway, I know the dorms are locking up soon, so I'll let you go. Thanks again for helping those boys."

Theron just waved goodbye in response and began walking out of the dining hall. On his way to the dorm, he noticed a shadow to his right. When he turned his attention to the shadow it retreated back into the forest, just barely viewable. Theron turned to approach the shadow, but when he got closer the shadow retreated further away. Theron thought it looked like a person, so he followed to find out who had been watching him. After he was about fifty meters off the path the shadow seemed to vanish completely. Theron guessed he had scared it off and decided to continue on to the dorm, but he heard a muffled scream back in the direction of the medical facility.

Theron rushed to the location the sound had come from, half expecting the sight he came upon. The doctor, Trish Vaashti, wearing the black leather armor he had seen her wearing the first night they met, was holding a student up by his throat. The scene was still surreal, but this time Theron wasn't frozen in fear. Almost on instinct he focused his energy and lashed out at Trish. She noticed the attack coming and calmly leapt nearly ten meters away, still holding the student in her right hand. Now that the angle of light had changed, Theron noticed that he knew the student. It was the first year that had ran impossibly well against Jacques and Theron, but now his eyes weren't merely bloodshot, they glowed red. Theron wasn't sure what to make of that, but he couldn't just let someone die in front of him, so he lashed out again.

This time Trish was watching him carefully and struck out with her own energy, easily battering his attack away. "Stand down, Theron. You don't know what you're dealing with." She didn't look surprised or even upset that he had shown up. Not like she had the first time.

Theron shook his head. "I know you're a psychic vampire, and I know you're trying to harm someone."

Trish narrowed her eyes. "So, someone has been teaching you some things. I guess that explains how you've learned to attack with your abilities. I was careless. But Theron, you don't know the whole story. I would never hurt a human."

"Then how do you explain what you are doing now, and what about the first night we met?" Theron argued.

"Oh, so you're finally willing to admit that you know what happened that night? I'm glad to hear that. You need to understand, Theron, that these creatures aren't human: they're vampires. As if the glowing red eyes and superhuman abilities weren't enough of a giveaway. Which reminds me, what were you thinking using your powers like that to win a stupid competition?" Trish's tone had become exasperated, as if she were dealing with a child.

She wasn't worried about what Theron might do. She wasn't even angry at him, and for some reason that annoyed him. Theron decided to show her that he should be taken more seriously. "So you're killing your own kind?"

"Of course not. This guy is a sanguine vampire. He drinks blood. He is only capable of hurting people. My duty is to guard humans from beings like him." Trish explained.

"That sounds noble." Theron said slowly. He allowed some of his psychic guard to weaken.

"It's not noble, it's just necessary." Trish refuted Theron's statement, but she seemed to relax some as well.

At that moment Theron whipped a knife out of his pocket that he had been keeping ever since he learned what Trish was. At one point he had almost decided to stop wearing it because Trish had almost convinced him she wasn't a bad person, but thanks to Uma's advice he had kept holding on to it. Now he released it at Trish's hand. Trish didn't have time to react as the knife sank into her arm and her hand released the vampire she held. The vampire started running off as soon as he hit the ground.

"Stupid boy!" Trish screamed as she ripped the knife out of her arm and threw it at the sanguine vampire's legs. The blade didn't sink into flesh, but it still made the vampire stumbled. Trish rushed forward to catch the vampire. She immediately started drawing energy from the boy, and Theron could see the knife wound in Trish's arm start to close itself. Within moments, the amount of energy she was consuming became so great that it became visible as light. A light eerily similar to what had come out of the boy she had consumed on that first night. Within the space of a few seconds the light winked out. Trish turned on Theron. "Do not interfere with things you know nothing about! I should just kill you and be done with it."

At least Theron has succeeded in making Trish angry. "If you try to kill me you'll just prove you're a liar. After all, you said you would never hurt a human."

At that comment the anger seemed to cool from Trish's eyes, and it was replaced by what looked like pity. "You still don't know do you? They haven't told you."

"What do you mean?" Theron asked, not understanding what Trish could be talking about.

Within the space of a breath Trish was suddenly in front of Theron. She gave him a sharp blow combined with a psychic attack he hadn't been ready for.

"Consider this payback," Trish told Theron as everything started going black. The last sensation that came to him was the feeling of Trish catching him as he started to fall.

Chapter 7

Truth

Theron awoke with his arms strapped down to a chair. He was in a room similar to his own dorm room. It was slightly larger and contained a small kitchen area, but otherwise the layout was the same. He was having trouble focusing his thoughts. It was difficult to concentrate, but his eyes were able to focus on one thing in the room: a woman sitting on the bed about two meters away from him.

Trish noticed Theron's gaze. "I see you're awake."

"So you decided to let me live after all. What are you going to do now?" Theron asked. He doubted she would just let him go.

"We are going to have a nice long chat," Trish said. "You probably don't realize this, but what you just saw was a setup designed to turn you against me."

"You can't expect me to believe that you're being framed," Theron said flatly.

"No, I wasn't framed. I meant that the situation was created specifically for you to see. The first time you saw me was too, but I didn't know it at the time," Trish explained.

"Why would someone do that? And by your words, I assume you mean you knew this time was a setup beforehand, so why would you participate?" Theron asked doubtfully.

Trish thought for a moment before answering, "I'll answer the second question first. Yes, I knew the situation was a trap. I don't know if you noticed, but I wasn't really surprised to see you happen upon the scene this time. Honestly, I wanted you to see it."

"Why?" Theron didn't understand at all.

"Because as long as we pretend that you don't remember the first time you saw me, we will be unable to move forward. We need to have an honest discussion, and I thought the best way to start that discussion was to spring the trap and force our little charade to an end," Trish answered.

"What do we have to discuss? You're a monster. You murder other beings just to sustain your own life," Theron accused. "No, what you do is worse than simple murder. You consume people's souls."

"First off, I want you to understand that I don't kill 'just' for the energy I gain," Trish clarified. "I kill sanguine vampires to protect humans, and that's part of what we need to discuss. Secondly, I don't actually consume souls. Granted, I do absorb a very large portion of my victims' energy, so much that they can no longer sustain their physical bodies, but the soul itself remains, much as a skeleton remains when all the flesh is removed from the physical body. Anyway, it's obvious someone has been giving you some information, but you don't know the whole story. Your understanding of what's really going on is so fragmented you can only reach false conclusions. I want you to think about the reason someone might want you to see me attack a student. I want you to consider the reason someone would want to turn you against me.

"This second show was probably set up because you and I were starting to get along, and they wanted to give you a reminder about what I really was. As I said, I decided to play along with the setup this time as part of a gamble. Maybe things will turn out in their favor. Maybe you and I will become enemies. But I decided to spring the trap for a chance to give you the truth. Listen to my side of the story before you demonize me. I really don't want to fight you Theron, and because I don't want to fight you, we need to have this conversation."

"I was told you have the ability to influence emotions. How can I trust you? For all I know you could have manipulated my feelings to make me like you." Theron objected.

"You've obviously been learning to use your psychic abilities. Tell me, have you learned to view energy yet?" Trish asked.

"Yes, if I concentrate," Theron answered. "But for some reason I can't seem to focus very well right now."

"I'm sorry about that," Trish apologized. "I gave you a drug that would prevent you from focusing well enough to control your abilities. I don't know how much you've been taught, and I didn't want you to escape, but I guess I'll have to gamble on that too. I'll give you something that should clear your head, or would you prefer to just wait for the effects of the drug to pass?"

"I'll wait. I guess it's normal to do what you must to keep a prisoner from escaping, but why are you going to let me regain the use of my abilities after going through the trouble making sure I couldn't use them?" Theron asked.

"If you're afraid I'm manipulating your emotions then I need to prove my innocence," Trish answered. "In order to have an honest conversation both parties have to be able to believe each other. If you concentrate and watch how I use my energy, you'll know whether or not I'm tampering with your emotions. I don't have anything to fear on that front. I've never tried to influence your feelings with my abilities. Actually, I don't think it would work even if I did try."

Theron gave Trish a questioning look. "What makes you say that?"

"I wasn't able to erase your memories, and I don't think you had received any training at that point," Trish explained. "That means you have some innate psychic defenses. I suspect those defenses would prevent anyone from psychically influencing you."

Trish's logic felt correct to Theron. Something within him let him know that she was right. "If it's innate then it doesn't require my concentration, correct?" Theron saw Trish nod. "In that case I'll believe you. What is your side of the story?"

Trish blinked a few times in surprise. "Thank you for believing me. I guess I should start from the beginning. I'm going to tell you an honest history as I have heard it. I'll tell you what I know about why both kinds of vampires were created, and why we are fighting. This will be a long story. We've been fighting for over four thousand years after all."

"I'm not going anywhere," Theron said as he pulled lightly on the restraints.

"That's true, I can take those off before I start if you like," Trish offered. Theron just shrugged, but Trish came over and loosened his restraints. "Trust should go both ways," Trish explained. "You said you would believe I'm not trying to psychically influence you, so I will believe that you'll listen to what I have to say without trying to escape. Do you need anything before I start?"

"Actually, if it's going to be a long story, I have to ask something else first or I probably won't be able to give your words my full attentions. What's with that leather armor? I'm not saying it doesn't look great on you, but it makes it seem like you're about to go to a renaissance festival." Theron answered.

Trish laughed. "I guess it does seem a bit out of place these days. It wasn't all that odd for warriors on foot to wear leather armor when I was young. Oddity aside though, for a psychic vampire, leather armor is the superior choice for protection. You see, leather is an organic material. Since it came from the skin of a once living creature, it is able to interact with our psychic energy. That means we can imbue it with supernatural properties. Modern armor uses synthetic materials, so I can't reinforce it with my power. On the other hand, I've made the leather armor I'm wearing impenetrable. It can also absorb heavy impacts and is capable of bending light if I want it to, making it excellent camouflage as well.

"While I'm on the topic of apparel, I noticed you don't seem to wear any silver. If you intend to continue your training, you should start wearing some, the purer the better."

Theron looked at Trish with a puzzled expression. "Why?"

"Have you ever heard the superstitions that silver weapons are the only thing that can kill a werewolf, or that silver is one of a vampire's weaknesses?" Theron nodded. He had done some research on the topic of vampire weaknesses since coming to New Babel Academy. "Well, it's indirectly true. High purity silver is the best natural conductor of electricity known. It also happens to have strong reactions with the spiritual energy we use. It can effectively paralyze our energy if it enters our bloodstream.

"However, it can also be attuned to a being's energy, allowing it to serve as an anchor and physical restraint. The more deeply you delve into your energy body, the weaker your connection to your physical body becomes. The more powerful abilities of our kind require us to delve very deeply into our energy bodies, so deep that our consciousness no longer resides in our physical forms. Without an anchor, this can be extremely dangerous, and we would no longer be able to use our physical bodies, but silver allows a psychic vampire to bind their souls to their bodies so that we can keep our consciousness in our energy body but still retain control over a physical actions. The physical body moves to keep up with the motions of the energy body. This also allows us to move beyond normal physical limitations."

Theron thought back to the time he had transferred his own consciousness into his energy body. He couldn't even imagine what might be possible if he could maintain that state while still having control of his physical body. "I'll look into getting some."

Trish nodded. "Is there anything else before I begin telling you about our history?" Theron shook his head. Trish took a breath and began her story. "Long ago, a race of beings, known as the Anunaki, guided the course of human history. These beings were worshiped as gods by the humans of that time, and under the watch of these powerful beings, the human race flourished in relative peace. We do not know where the Anunaki came from, but we do know that their way of guiding humanity went unopposed until about forty-five hundred years ago. At that time a young Anunaki challenged his elders' methods, and everything began to fall apart.

"You see, the Anunaki had the power to completely dominate the human race, but they chose not to. Instead, they decided to simply watch over humans. They controlled the elements and created an environment where humanity could grow and flourish. They established teachings to form a moral authority for the people and create a blueprint for civilization, but, with a few exceptions, they did not interfere with the choices humans made. They allowed humans to rebel and fight one another, though they would intervene if conflicts began to grow too large. They willingly took a background role to support the lives of humans, allowing the human race to take center stage.

"I've been told that the young Anunaki I mentioned couldn't accept the role his elders took in supporting humans. He believed that humans were defective because they were incapable of governing themselves. He observed that humanity, when left to its own devices, inevitably became self-destructive. Human greed and laziness caused them to kill and enslave one another. With few exceptions, they sought the easiest life possible, even at the cost of their self-worth and pride. They would always seek to avoid responsibility and blame others if they did something wrong, or if life grew harsh for them. In short, this young Anunaki came to view humans as despicable creatures unworthy of the care and attention the older Anunaki lavished upon them. He began to argue that the Anunaki should either rule over human kind directly in an attempt to correct their enormous flaws, or destroy humanity completely.

"Most of his elders refused to accept the position of the young Anunaki, and a growing feeling of animosity began to develop. To make matters worse, this Anunaki was incredibly powerful, even among his own kind. I've been told his power was enough to rival even the leader of the Anunaki, Marduk. Because of his greater power and unyielding will, the young Anunaki eventually decide to take matters into his own hands. He decided to personally end the human race and declared he would destroy any who opposed his goals. That declaration marked the beginning of the War of Perdition. The young Anunaki also earned a new name: Qayinus, which marked him as the successor to the biblical Cain.

"The Anunaki that had agreed with Qayinus or who feared his power and decided to join him in hopes of gaining greater status for themselves went over to his side. Still, a majority of the Anunaki remained united against him under the rule of Marduk, and the two sides became locked in a stalemate. Qayinus was too strong, and the older Anunaki were unwilling to kill him. On the other hand, the other Anunaki were too numerous for Qayinus to overpower them and accomplish his goal. Eventually, Qayinus decided he had to increase his forces, but he needed to retain as much of his strength as possible for the battle with the other Anunaki, so he decided to create six hybrid beings. These beings would have powers far beyond a human's, but they wouldn't be nearly as strong as an Anunaki. Qayinus hoped that they would be able to pass the Anunaki's defenses unnoticed and act as assassins.

"Qayinus took six human children and raised them, shaping them into tools of war. He showed them all the cruelty humans were capable of, and over time warped their minds so that they hated their own kind. After he was satisfied that the minds of these six humans, now adults, were completely devoted to his goals, Qayinus and five other Anunaki that had joined him performed a ritual. Each one of the Anunaki transferred some of their tremendous power to one of the six. The power began to alter the souls of the six, and the effects started to spill over and change their physical bodies as well. I have been told that if Qayinus and his followers had completed the ritual, the six would have been completely transformed into Anunaki, but they chose to end the ritual early. He left the six trapped in an existence between human and Anunaki. The result was everything Qayinus had intended with one additional side effect: an irresistible demand for more energy to complete the transformation. That demand for energy could only be met by absorbing the life energy of souled creatures. Since the souls and bodies of the six weren't sufficiently changed for them to manifest psychic abilities, the only way for them to absorb the energy they needed was through drinking blood, which is the medium containing a being's life energy. Qayinus had succeeded in creating the first sanguine vampires.

"The new vampires performed better than Qayinus had hoped. They were easily able to blend in with ordinary humans and avoid detection. Their irresistible desire for energy caused them to gorge themselves on the blood of humans. It wasn't long before Qayinus began an experiment. He ordered his vampire tools to attack the Anunaki directly. The Anunaki didn't suspect a thing. When one would come to investigate a slaughter caused by a vampire, the vampire would act as a survivor and get close enough to drain the blood and kill the Anunaki. Luckily, absorbing energy by consuming blood is actually very inefficient, so most of the energy was wasted. If the vampires had gained the full power of each Anunaki they killed, the world would be a very different place. The older Anunaki would have lost.

"For a time, the Anunaki were completely at a loss to explain the death of their comrades. They weren't even sure what was causing the deaths because the vampires never left survivors to bear witness to their deeds. But eventually the problem solved itself in a way. As the vampires absorbed more energy, their transformations progressed and they began to produce an inhuman presence that the Anunaki could detect. Of course, even though the Anunaki could detect the vampires, they still didn't have any idea what they were, so none of the vampires were killed at that time, but they also weren't able to carry out their mission to kill humans and the more wary Anunaki. The six vampires lost their effectiveness as assassins.

"In response to the growing power of his tools and their new vulnerability to detection, Qayinus decided to perform a new experiment. He ordered the six vampires to kidnap humans and turn them against humanity by any means necessary. I don't know how they did it exactly, but they succeeded. After confirming that the human prisoners would become good additional tools to accomplish his goals, he ordered the six vampires to feed the humans their own blood until they turned into vampires themselves. The second generation of sanguine vampires was created, and because they were weaker than their progenitors, they could avoid detection by the Anunaki.

"At this time, Qayinus made his biggest mistake. He assumed that the new vampires would be able to continue where the primogens, the first generation vampires, had stopped. He ordered the young vampires to attack the Anunaki, but they were weaker than their sires had been when they were first created, and they hadn't even been able to gain energy from feeding on humans first. As a result, the new vampires were only a little stronger than a normal human, so when they attacked the Anunaki, in spite of their element of surprise, they weren't able to kill them. Instead, the vampires were captured. The Anunaki were finally able to resolve the mysteries of what had been happening.

"The Anunaki carefully interrogated and studied the vampires they caught and were able to figure out how they had been created. They learned about the strengths and weaknesses of vampires as a race, and they learned that different vampires had different talents and inclinations that were based on which primogen had sired them. The Anunaki determined that all vampires fell into one of six bloodlines, which is how we know there are six primogens. They further theorized that each primogen had been created with the energy of traitor Anunaki from each of the six houses that made up the Anunaki: House Amitheir, House Vaash, House Orinthal, House Nah'radine, House Sevit, and House Meishar.

"Much of what the Anunaki learned was fairly academic, but they were shocked by the discovery that the vampires could absorb and assimilate the life energy of other beings. The Anunaki themselves didn't possess that ability. They could channel energy, but they couldn't absorb it. The Anunaki immediately realized the grave threat the vampires posed. The vampires blended in with humans too well, and the Anunaki wouldn't start indiscriminately slaughtering humans just to kill a vampire. In contrast, the immense energy of the Anunaki allowed vampires to instantly detect them, making the Anunaki vulnerable to surprise attack. The Anunaki realized they needed tools of their own to counter the vampires Qayinus had created.

"At that time, Marduk, who had tried not to get too involved with the war for some reason, finally decided to act. He took all the research on vampires and came up with a plan. He gathered together six humans with compassionate hearts, strong wills, and unerring devotion to the beings they worshiped as gods. Marduk then gathered the strongest Anunaki from each of the six houses and with their aid reproduced the ritual

Qayinus had enacted to create the sanguine vampires. Marduk allowed the ritual to continue for a longer time than Qayinus had, theorizing that a more complete transformation would create a stronger and more stable form of vampire. When the ritual stopped and the new beings were examined, it was discovered that the six beings also possessed the ability to absorb and assimilate energy, and because of their more complete transformation, they also manifested psychic abilities. They became the first psychic vampires, and they were the first line of defense against the sanguine vampires of Qayinus.

"The six psychic vampires suffered from the same demand for life energy that the sanguine vampires had, but their psychic abilities allowed them to siphon small amounts of energy directly from another beings soul, rather than having to ingest blood. That meant they could feed from people without harming them, as the energy they took would replenish itself with time. When the psychic vampires began to hunt the sanguine vampires, the real differences between them became immediately apparent. Since sanguine vampires didn't have psychic abilities, their sensitivity to the energy levels of other beings was actually very poor. They could sense an Anunaki because they were so overwhelmingly powerful that it was impossible not to, even normal humans could sense that power after all, but the sanguine vampires couldn't differentiate between the psychic vampires and humans. The psychic vampires didn't suffer from that weakness. Their well-developed psychic abilities and energy manipulation techniques allowed them to easily detect sanguine vampires.

"The psychic vampires were easily able to fight the sanguine vampires, but ultimately the war was only brought back to a stalemate. You see, the Anunaki were greatly tormented by what they were forced to do. They hated the fact they had to create the psychic vampires. That's not to say they hated the psychic vampires themselves. Indeed, from what I've heard the Anunaki felt indebted to the beings that had to sacrifice their humanity in order to fight on the Anunaki's behalf, but they didn't want to cause any more harm than they already had, so they forbid the creation of more psychic vampires. Meanwhile, the original six sanguine vampires hid behind all the vampires they sired, sending their children out to be slaughtered. No primogen was killed during that time, and the war stayed in a deadlock until about four thousand years ago.

"Eventually, Marduk grew weary and felt crushed by guilt for what the Anunaki were doing. He still believed humans were the ones that should have mastery over the Earth, so he couldn't surrender to Qayinus. Instead Marduk came up with a final solution to the war, but it would demand the sacrifice of the Anunaki civilization. In preparation for this, Marduk began to reorganize humanity. Up until this point, human kingdoms were centered around individual city-states, and no war was allowed to get so far out of hand that another city state would perish. Marduk now allowed city-states to conquer one another. He allowed the creation of the Akkadian Empire under Sargon the Great. Marduk hoped uniting humanity under a strong human ruler would allow them to live without the support of the Anunaki.

"Of course, Marduk, like Qayinus, understood that human hearts and minds were flawed to the point that they would destroy one another over the most insignificant things. Humans would always ultimately prove unable to govern themselves over any significant period of time, so Marduk began establishing new cities and bringing other older cities to greater prominence, hoping that if the empire failed, the strong position of other cities would allow a new center of government to rise up and bring order to humanity again. It might seem like a terrible way to view the humans he was supposed to protect, but to Marduk, the war was never about a disagreement on the nature of mankind. It was about what role the Anunaki should play in human life.

"Originally, Marduk had believed that the Anunaki, being immortal and far more powerful, should protect and guide humans, but the War of Perdition had taught him a lesson. The Anunaki were no better than humans, they were just a smaller community. The lack of diversity had made them appear more harmonious, and had deceived them all into thinking they were more enlightened than humans. With that realization, Marduk resolved to stop pretending he was a god. He decided to stop interfering with human lives, and bring an end to the Anunaki civilization. He convinced his subjects to follow his beliefs, and gave his final orders to the psychic vampires. We still follow those final orders to this day. They are the oaths we live by.

"All psychic vampires swear to pass on their life and power within no more than five hundred years of receiving them. That power is to be given to human successors that will carry on the oaths of their predecessors. The only exception to that rule is the psychic vampire Pazuzu. His oath was to become a living chronicle of the truth, the historian of the ages. We all also swear to not interfere with the fate of humanity, except when we are trying to prevent interference from another supernatural being. We swear to protect humanity from the shadows. We protect them from all the mistakes and evils caused by the pride of the Anunaki, including the surviving sanguine vampires. Finally, we swear to live among humans, not to rule over them or guide them, but to be their friends and companions. If any psychic vampire breaks their vows, the others will capture him, find a suitable successor, and force that vampire to give over his life and power."

"After Marduk gave the psychic vampires those oaths to swear, he gathered together all the Anunaki under his command and performed a great ritual. Marduk had studied the energy draining abilities of vampires enough to create this ritual. Its power reached out across the world and sought out Qayinus and his Anunaki followers. It grabbed hold of them and ripped their energy from them and sealed it away. The final part of the ritual transported Qayinus and his followers, now reduced to the power of normal humans but still possessing immortal bodies, to remote locations around the world. They were locked away and kept from ever being able to reach out and influence the human world again. When the ritual was finished, the Anunaki with Marduk collapsed, and one by one they started dying. They didn't have enough energy remaining to sustain their bodies anymore. Marduk was the last to die, and with his final breath, he delivered a prophecy. He declared that humanity would grow to one day cover the Earth, and in time, Qayinus would be loosed upon the world again by mortal hands. Before that day came, Marduk would return to face Qayinus, and at that time he would harden his heart. If Qayinus still sought to carry out his goals, Marduk would not spare him again.

"Then Marduk died, and the age of the Anunaki came to an end. The psychic vampires kept true to their word. To this day, we fight against the sanguine vampires. We do not interfere with the choices of humanity, and we weep at the consequences or take joy in the result of those choices alongside our human friends, not judging them, but living with them. Over the millennia, we have added a few more rules to the oaths Marduk gave us, like we are not allowed to have children because they will be born as sanguine vampires. That was learned through experience shortly after the fall of the Anunaki.

"We really haven't done a whole lot though. We kill sangs, that's short for sanguine vampires, by the way. We kill them when we find them, but in all this time we have never managed to kill a primogen. The Anunaki are all gone, but we left over tools continue their fight for dominion. After all, it's what we were made for and all we're really good at. The War of Perdition is much more subdued now, but it is still ongoing in what feels like eternal deadlock, though that may change soon." Trish gave Theron a meaningful look and fell silent. Her long story was finally finished.

Theron thought through everything Trish had told him. To his surprise he found himself believing the story. In fact, it almost felt familiar to him. He had felt something within him almost nodding in agreement as Trish told the story. He felt compelled to accept the events described as the truth. He started to wonder if Trish had done something to him after all, but the thought felt wrong. Trish had simply told him the story, nothing more. What Theron did with that knowledge was now up to him.

"May I ask a few questions?" Theron asked. Trish nodded in response. "You said several times that you were told this story, and given the oath to live no more than five hundred years, I assume this is second hand knowledge at best."

"You are correct. I wasn't there. I'm not even two centuries old yet. My sire wasn't there for it either, but he was the first one to tell me the story when I was still a human. Later, after I became a psychic vampire, I heard the story again from Pazuzu, and he really was there, so I think it's safe to say it's accurate to the best of our knowledge."

Theron nodded. "I understand you don't mean humans any harm and that you believe killing sanguine vampires is the right thing to do, but my question is: how can you be sure all sanguine vampires are bad? I believe the events you've told me about really did happen, but can we say for certain that the sanguine vampires today are just as opposed to humanity as they were then? If it's all based on what you've been told by other psychic vampires, how do you know it isn't just some long standing indoctrination designed to keep the war going."

Trish looked at Theron with a small smile, but her eyes were sad. "I had my doubts when I was younger, and not just about the nature of the sanguine vampires, but about the truth of the history as well. I think anyone would question the idea that an entire group could be that evil, but you have to remember sangs aren't a random collection of individuals. Each and every one of them has been hand-picked. They have been conditioned to hate humans. I mentioned I don't know how the sangs do it, but I've seen the results. I've seen humans who were good, kind, and loving people get turned into sanguine vampires and then smile with delight as they ripped someone's heart out. And even if they weren't evil, sangs can't resist their bodies demand for energy. Even if they weren't conditioned to hate humans, they would still attack humans like a rabid animal. They were created entirely to be perfect human killing machines. Even if one did manage to retain their human heart and mind, you would be doing them a favor by killing them."

"I see." Theron frowned. He didn't disbelieve Trish, but he also couldn't accept her answer. "I'll be honest, I can't just accept that from your words. I don't really doubt you, but I think it might be something that each person has to see for themselves. That being said, if you're right, I hope I never have to see it."

Trish nodded. "Because I once thought the same thing, I understand what you're saying. I won't try to force you to act on my beliefs. You will find that I've told you the truth on your own. It's not something you can avoid."

Theron took on a puzzled expression as he looked at Trish. "What do you mean? I guess that ties into my next question: why are you telling me this at all?"

"Because for over four thousand years there have only been six psychic vampires alive at any given time, but now there are seven," Trish told Theron in an even tone.

Theron was filled with apprehension. "Seven?

"Theron, the reason the sangs wanted you to turn against me, and the reason I'm telling you the whole truth so that you will consider helping me, is because you are a psychic vampire. You were born as a psychic vampire. It's something that should be impossible. It's never happened before, and I have no idea how it has happened now, but here you are."

Theron shook his head. "I'm a psychic vampire? That can't be true. I mean, I know I have psychic abilities, but a vampire?"

Trish looked at him with eyes filled with suffering. Theron knew she didn't want to tell him what she was about to say. "Theron, this won't be easy for you to hear, but it's the truth. I've confirmed it by looking at your medical records, the case of your parent's unknown disease, and the medical records of children at the orphanage you grew up in. You were born with a severely weakened body because your energy was barely enough to support your body. You suffered the same symptom that a vampire suffers when they don't feed for an extended period of time. Because you have innate psychic abilities, you began to subconsciously feed on those around you. That's why you "miraculously" recovered from your weak condition and continued to grow in strength."

"Hold on," Theron interrupted before Trish could continue. His mind had taken on a tinge of desperation, trying to refute the conclusion of what Trish had told him. "I just learned how to feed on energy recently. I was told that I only started to feed on people subconsciously after I learned to do it consciously."

Trish shook her head. "No Theron. You're a psychic vampire. Psychic feeding is an innate ability. It doesn't need to be taught. You can learn to consciously direct it, but the actual act will occur naturally. In essence, a psychic vampire doesn't learn how to feed; they have to learn how to stop feeding to ensure they don't inadvertently bring harm to others."

The words hit Theron hard. He knew they were true. He felt it in the deepest parts of his being. "Then, my parents?"

Trish's eyes were filled with sympathy, but she answered in a level tone, "They were drained of energy to the point of death due to continuous close proximity to you. Likewise, the children at your orphanage had generally poor health and fitness and grew sick far more than is normal for children in similar situations. The longer a child stayed at the orphanage, the worse those symptoms became. Luckily, due to the number of children and the transient nature of living in an orphanage, not many of them were exposed long enough to develop the more severe complications long term feeding can cause."

"I killed my parents." The life seemed to slowly drain out of Theron's eyes as the truth settled in his mind. He didn't sob, and he didn't even blink as tears began to gather and silently slide down his cheeks. His voice was lifeless when he finally managed to voice his thoughts. "I'm a monster."

Trish walked over to Theron and embraced him. "I'm so sorry Theron. But you need to remember what I said to you before when you first told me what happened to your parents. You couldn't help it. You were simply too young and inexperienced to do anything about it. I meant it, everything that happened up until now was beyond your control. Besides, think about your parents. It's clear how much they must have loved you by how much you still love them. If they were given the choice to die so that their son would live, what do you think they would have done?"

Theron finally blinked. Trish's words sounded nice, but they didn't do anything to alleviate the crushing guilt he felt. "But it wasn't their choice."

"It wasn't yours either," Trish told Theron firmly. "It just happened. It's the same as getting struck by lightning. No one is to blame for it. All you can do is keep their memory in your heart and live the best you can. Try to be the kind of person they would have wanted you to be. Don't let their memory become a burden, instead let it be a wind at your back, pushing you forward and holding you on a righteous path. That is the only way their deaths can have meaning. Otherwise it would just be a senseless random death, but even then it wouldn't be your fault." Theron shook his head. He couldn't bring himself to accept Trish's words.

She's right. It's not your fault; it's mine. Theron froze as the thought entered his mind. The thought wasn't his. It reminded him of the thought he had heard when he had deeply mediated under the chairwoman's guidance weeks ago. The voice of the thought matched the one that had told him he wasn't ready to completely enter his mind.

Who are you? What do you mean? Theron tried to send his thoughts to the voice, but there was no response.

Trish had no idea what was going on in Theron's mind, but she continued to try to comfort him. "You may not be able to accept what I'm telling you right away. I know all of this is very sudden for you, but you have to pull through this. I'm here for you if you need me. I'll do anything I can to help you understand you have nothing to feel guilty about. I'll teach you to control your abilities so nothing like that happens again. I'll be a friend that you can tell everything to. Let me support you."

"I'm sorry." Theron told Trish. He gently pulled her arms off him. "I need time. I need to think through all this. I know in my mind what you're telling me is right, but I need time to convince my heart. Once that's done, I'll think about what I need to do about your war, if anything. I don't feel right asking anything more from you until after I've made my decision about that."

Trish shut her eyes tightly. She almost looked a little lonely and hurt that he wasn't relying on her. "I understand. But please remember, I mean it with all my heart when I say I'm here for you if you need me."

Theron nodded. "Thank you Trish. I'm going to go back to my room now."

Trish only nodded in response as Theron turned to leave. The door was unlocked, which Theron found a little surprising given that he had been held captive. It was still dark out as he started walking back to his dorm. The moon was hidden by the mountains, but the lights along the path kept things well lit. Theron was reminded of the first night he had met Trish. It was the last time he had walked alone at night on the well-lit paths. When he got about halfway back to the dorm, he noticed a person leaning up against one of the solar lamps. Theron recognized the figure as Deacon.

"I must say, I didn't really expect things to turn out like this," Deacon said as he pushed himself off the pole. As Deacon got further from the light, Theron noticed his eyes were red.

"Deacon, you're a —"

"A sanguine vampire. Yes." Deacon finished Theron's sentence and gave a confirmation. "In truth, I'm surprised you're alive. I was also surprised when you attacked Doctor Vaashti, but even more so that she let you live."

"How do you know about that?" Theron narrowed his eyes as he questioned Deacon.

Deacon shrugged. "I set up the encounter between her and the vampire she killed earlier, and I was watching. I saw her knock you out and take you away. I've been waiting here for you since."

"Why?" Theron questioned.

"I wanted to remind you about what she is. I thought it would end up like the first time, but I underestimated you. Now that she's revealed herself to you, I'm forced to do the same. I'm in charge of the vampires on this campus, so I'm going to be their representative and make an appeal for your help in stopping Trish," Deacon told Theron.

Theron narrowed his eyes again. "So now you're trying to recruit me openly instead of trying to manipulate me. You say you're in charge, but is Uma in on your scheme?"

Deacon shook his head. "The chairwoman doesn't know about us. Though I did make sure the right documents appeared on her desk so she could identify Doctor Vaashti as a psychic vampire. She's just being manipulated too. We sanguine vampires are pretty easily killed by our psy vamp cousins, so we tend to try to hide in the shadows and use pawns to do most of our work. I do apologize for trying to manipulate you as well, but I hope you understand that we were just trying to protect ourselves."

"I can understand that," Theron said hesitantly. "But why should I side with you over Trish? Not that I've decided to join the other psychic vampires either."

"Ah, so you know that you're one of them now," Deacon stated. Theron nodded. "Good, it means we can start teaching you more powerful abilities now that you won't have to deal with the illusion of your humanity. As for your question, the answer is simple: siding with us is in the best interest of the world."

Theron had to ask Deacon, "You knew I was a psychic vampire. Did you know about my parents?"

Deacon sighed. "So you figured that out too. I'm sorry to hear that. I would have tried to spare your feelings. Yes, I knew you were responsible for their death. But it's nothing to feel bad about. It's a simple case of survival of the fittest. Your parents died because they got too close to a superior being and were consumed. It's tragic, but if you think about it like that, it happens all the time. Still, you have my sympathy."

Theron was shocked by Deacon's analysis, but he narrowed his eyes at Deacon's expression of sympathy. "You say it's tragic they died, but don't you want to kill all humans anyway?" Theron accused Deacon.

Deacon shook his head. "That was only a last resort a long time ago as I understand it. That was back when the gods were fighting over what to do with humans. Now that the gods aren't around to interfere, we don't have to resort to those kinds of drastic measures. We want to help keep them from making mistakes. We want to ensure they stop killing each other. We want them to learn to treat one another and their environment with respect and kindness. We want to help them overcome their selfish natures. I grant you that the measures necessary to improve the nature of humans will be harsh at first, but they will make everything so much better for everybody in the long run. The perfect form of government isn't a democracy, as most of the world seems to think today. The perfect form of government is actually a dictatorship under the rule of a perfect dictator. Even simply a good and righteous dictator would be a huge step up from most of the selfish and corrupt leaders in the world today. Don't you think?"

Theron couldn't refute Deacon's words. Humans as a species did an awful lot of terrible things to one another. It was also true that all governments ultimately failed. Weak governments fell to outside forces, while strong governments that managed to protect themselves ultimately grew corrupt and fell apart from within. A quick study of history could easily lead one to the conclusion that humans weren't fit to govern themselves. At that point, one would normally just shrug and say there was no other alternative, but was that really the case? What would a group of immortal rulers be like? If they were beings of noble character and strong will, could they resist the fate that had befallen so many other rulers? Such people were exceedingly rare, which is probably why dynasties ultimately failed since they couldn't continuously produce good rulers, but if one such person were immortal how long could they be a good, benevolent leader?

Deacon smiled at Theron's silence. "It doesn't sound so bad, right? We're not evil. Did you know we don't even kill humans anymore? Even when we need to feed, we find willing donors and only feed on small amounts of blood at a time. Actually the explosion in popularity of fictional vampires has made our lives much easier in that regard. Humans actually like sanguine vampires. Of course, we don't have a lot in common with those works of fiction. We're not undead at all, more like superhuman. We can have children. We can be out in sunlight. We are immortal as long as we continue to absorb energy. Stakes, silver, and garlic don't do a thing to us. Well, actually garlic may give us gas, but it seems to be on an individual basis." Deacon grinned a little wider as he cracked his joke.

Theron sighed. "I guess it's only natural that both sides believe they are doing the right thing. Everyone is the hero of their own story, and everyone who opposes them is the villain. But that means that I can't just decide which side I will choose based upon your words alone. I need to be able to observe both sides acting on their beliefs. I need to see the results of their efforts. I can only choose a side when I know which one's methods and ideals I agree with, and that will take time. I can't decide right away."

Deacon nodded. "So basically everything will continue as before. Well, I'll introduce you to some other sanguine vampires and let you in on some of our activities. I can't tell you everything of course in case you turn into an enemy, but I'll show you as much as I can to help you make your decision. I think you'll come to understand that we're actually the good guys. That's about all I have to say for now, so I'll see you around." Deacon waved and walked off the path, within moments he had disappeared into the night.

Theron was feeling numb. He had been overloaded with too many revelations. He needed time to sort everything out. Eventually he would have to make a choice between helping the sanguine vampires achieve their vision for the world or helping the psychic vampires rid the world of the sanguine vampires' influence, but he couldn't make the decision now. He would have to observe Trish and Deacon carefully from now on, but that could wait until tomorrow. For right now, he wanted to go to his room and curl up in a ball. He knew when his numbness faded he'd start thinking of his parents again. He didn't want anyone else to see him while he did.

* * * * *

"So, you revealed your true nature to Theron." The chairwoman frowned at the kneeling Student Council President. She was clearly upset by what she had just learned.

Deacon kept his head bowed as he responded, "Yes my lady. I realized Trish Vaashti had captured him to reveal her true nature, and her motivations behind killing us. I had to give Theron an opposing view. At least now it'll be a fair choice. I was also able to protect your identity, so in the worst case you could still kill him without him suspecting anything."

The chairwoman sighed. "I guess it can't be helped. You actions were correct. This entire night has just been unfortunate."

"I shall try to show Theron our best face going forward," Deacon assured the chairwoman.

She shook her head slightly. "No, you can't do that. If he were to make a choice based only on our best nature he would be a constant threat of turning against us as he got more involved. You must try to thoroughly indoctrinate him. He must be convinced that even our most brutal methods are justified. You can pull him in slowly. Start out with showing him less unpleasant activities, but do not actually hide anything. Now go and prepare with the others. Make sure everyone understands how important this is."

"As you wish, my lady." Deacon rose to his feet and turned to leave.

Once he was gone, the chairwoman looked out the window. She could see the sky beginning to lighten. The night was almost over. The chairwoman gently whispered to herself, "Lord Qayinus, I may have to awaken you sooner than I planned."

The End of the First Book of The Anunaki Saga

Author's Note

To everyone reading this: nice to meet you. My name is Gavin Teague and I'd like to thank you for taking the time to read *Tools of Dominion: Truth*, the first book of The Anunaki Saga. Seeing as this is the first opportunity any of you have had to read my work, I'd like to take a couple pages to write a little about some of my inspirations and share a few details about my writing methods that may shed some light on the mythos I'm building with this story

Over the past few years, I've been pretty strongly influenced by some forms of Japanese media, especially light novels, which are much more serialized than what most Americans are probably used to. With that in mind, I decided that I'd use a shorter, more serialized format to my own books in the hope that I'll be able to write a couple of books each year. Following that goal, I plan on releasing the next book of the series, *Tools of Dominion: Choice*, in mid-December, 2014.

As for my writing style, I like writing in layers. By that, I mean I try to write my stories so people can just sit down and read the story and enjoy it at face value, but at the same time, if someone really wants to delve into the story and find hidden meaning and implications, they can do that too. I also like to weave in hidden clues about what might happen in future books for people who like to make theories about what might happen to the characters. On that note, as a hint for those interested in theory crafting, a good place to start would be to look at the meaning of some of the characters' names. I should also mention that Theron's last name, Zeyla, is actually an American English phonetic adaptation of the German word Seele, meaning soul.

I also tend to spend a lot of time researching little details, most of which will never matter to you all as readers. For example, when deciding where New Babel Academy would be located geographically, I actually researched the rock composition of various sections of the Alps to find a plausible location that would contain the types of rocks I wanted to use in the buildings. It's probably overkill since this is fiction, but I had fun learning about that and a hundred other minor things, and if there is even one of you out there that enjoys some of those little bits of reality woven into the story, then I think it was time well spent.

Regarding the story itself, the backstory setting for The Anunaki Saga goes back about seven thousand years and creates a mythos that explains the origins of just about everything that we know of as supernatural in lore and legend. I'll introduce a few details of that backstory into the main narrative, like Trish revealing part of the history of the War of Perdition, but most of the details won't be talked about much in this series. Once I've published a few volumes I'll probably start releasing books that flesh out the backstory as a separate series, but we'll have to see how much time I have. Writing books for this series will be my main priority, and I may also discuss some of the backstory in the author's notes of future books.

With that, I'll bring this little monologue to a close. Thank you again for reading, and I hope to be able to write to you all again in a few months when the second book comes out.

- Gavin Teague

About the Author

Gavin Teague was born on Elmendorf Air Force Base in Alaska. He was raised and currently resides in Kansas. He has been and avid fan of science fiction and fantasy almost since he started reading.

Made in the USA
Charleston, SC
15 November 2014